DEDICATION

I dedicate this book to my foster father, Dr. S. Newton, whose love and guidance have made me all that I am today. Because of him, I learned to dream and to live my dreams.

I would also like to dedicate this book to my biological family, and all the people who never give up on their dreams.

-   Vasile Onica

ACKNOWLEDGMENTS

I have met some amazing people throughout my life. They all have contributed to my successes or failures in some way.

Every single experience has taught me something – I have learned something from everyone and every experience.

However, since I cannot name every single person in this book, I can name the ones who have really, really made a great impact to my life. Some names have been altered to respect their confidentiality.

I would like to thank, first and for most, my foster father: Dr. Stuart Newton, to whom I dedicate this book, and my three foster sisters – Nicola, Andrea and Natasha.

You have taught me how to dream and follow my dreams, the importance of self-acceptance, total integrity and utmost respect for myself as well as for others. Because of you I have managed to come to the stage of bringing this book into form.

I would like to thank my biological family too, for their unconditional love and support.

My appreciation goes to Miss. P Spencer and Mrs. R Hensor – you have made it possible for me to finish my University course, and I will always be grateful for your kindness and generosity.

I would like to say a big thank you to Jean Arkwright and her family, and Nicolae Iuga and his family – you are one of the kindest people I have met.

I could not have managed to cope with the physical demand of Mt. Kilimanjaro, so I thank my English best

…end, Watipa, for all the hours he dedicated to training me, both in and outside the gym. You are a true friend!

My best friends from Romania, Mircea Onac, his wife Andra and their beautiful son Alex, his sister Ioana, his brother Bogdan, his cousin Dana, and his parents: Mr and Mrs Onac. You guys have always been there for me, especially when things were tough – Thank you!

Last but not least, I would like to thank my Kilimanjaro team, in particular: Ritchie, Jo, Mark, Patriczja, Marianna, Joy, Nanas, Evelyn, Joni, Jemma, Louise, Boblar, Andy, my tent buddy Jamie, and everyone else at the travel company. I would also like to acknowledge the amazing help and support of the Tanzanian porters, they have been phenomenal. Because of you all, I have managed to reach the top of Mt. Kilimanjaro – you are all amazing and I appreciate the people you are.

It has been a great pleasure and honour to have met you and shared one of the most memorable moments of my life with you.

If I have missed anyone, I apologise, but know that everyone I have come into contact with has played a significant part in my life.

Thank you all, profoundly!

Introduction

I never really wanted to write a book, let alone tell people my life story, but after so many "what happened to you?" or "Vas you have climbed 2 mountains on crutches, you should tell people about it", I decided to give it a go. So, here I am. I will try to tell you my story in as much detail as I can remember; I will also try to tell you my experience of climbing two mountains on crutches.

So why did I write this book? It was for the following reasons:

1. To motivate people to say "if he can do it, so can I".
2. To encourage people to go out there and live life to the full.
3. To encourage people to never give up.
4. To understand how important, and beneficial, it is to forgive.
5. To show you how to overcome obstacles.
6. To show you how to keep a positive mental attitude, even when things do not work out the way you want them to.

I have done my best to make this book as motivating as possible, but I have also tried to keep it as natural as possible. I am telling you my story with as much information as I can remember. I hope you accept that I do not remember every experience I had in my life, with every single detail, and how I dealt with it, but I have tried to give you the bigger picture. I also hope that you will understand that English is not my first language, so some words or sentences might not make sense to you. I do apologise in advance, and I encourage you to keep on reading.

I would like to stress the fact that this book is not an autobiography. This is intended to be of a motivational nature, telling you my obstacles and my achievements and how I dealt with them.

This is a 3 part book: 1st part is about my early life in Romania. 2nd part is about my experiences when I moved to U.K. 3rd part is about my challenges of climbing Mt. Kilimanjaro and Mt Snowdon. However, in between I try not to just tell you my story, but to motivate you in some way as well.

So my wish is that you will enjoy reading this, but most of all, I truly hope that by reading it you will have realised that you can do, be and have anything you want in life. I truly and sincerely hope that this book will make a positive impact in your life.

I encourage you to believe in yourself, to believe in your dreams and to never give up if something doesn't work out in your life the way you wanted it to. Just remember, things happen for a good reason, you might not see the good reason now, but the time will come when you will see the positive in every negative experience. Everything happens for our highest good, so believe that you are meant to achieve great things, even if you have 'failed' at some things now. You are meant to succeed!

What is your dream? It doesn't matter how small or how ridiculous it might seem to someone else, it is your dream...dream it and achieve it. You have the power, the strength and the knowledge within yourself to achieve anything you put your mind to.

So, go out there and make your life a dream come true! If I can do it, you can do it too!

I look forward to hearing from you, but most of all I look forward to hearing that you have decided to follow your dream and make it a reality…

Sincerely, to your stellar success,

Vas

(Vasile Onica)

PART 1

MY EARLY LIFE

Chapter 1

A Mistake Was Made

"I think we all wish we could erase some dark times in our lives. But all of life's experiences, bad and good, make you who you are. Erasing any of life's experiences would be a great mistake." -
Luis Miguel

We all make mistakes, and whether they are big or small, they affect our lives in some way. At times, someone else makes a mistake and we have to pay the price for it. Some mistakes really do not make a great difference in life, and we just move on without a problem. But some apparently small mistakes have big effects. It was a mistake like that which left its mark on my life, and I will never be able to shake it off. It will stay with me for as long as I live.

In life we learn things through trial and error. When we make mistakes, we get hurt and we learn from the experience.

Learning by trial and error goes on throughout life – we learn the importance of trust when we are betrayed. We learn to understand love when our heart is broken. We learn to value things when we lose them. Mistakes really do teach us so much about the world we live in.

The building blocks of our lives are nothing but the mistakes we make. They make us stronger and teach us lessons that we keep going back to, for the rest of our lives. As infants, we struggle to get on our feet. We fall and hurt ourselves. But eventually, all those bruises and falls help us learn to walk. And that is exactly how we learn all of life's lessons. Our lives are shaped by our errors. And I started my life with one such mistake – only it was someone else's error that so profoundly affected my life.

In my hometown of Calarasi, in Romania, in November of 1980, it was mandatory for children aged six months to have a vaccination against polio and many other viruses. This vaccine was supposed to protect children from polio. On a cold, dark day in November, 1980, a tragic incident occurred that went unreported: 12 babies were given a contaminated injection by a nurse, who allegedly had just finished her training and was starting her first job. As a result, some of the babies were completely paralysed, and two died within a few days. Just one baby escaped with a "minor" problem, and was called "the lucky one." He had permanent damage to his left leg because some of the nerves to the muscles were killed as a result of that injection. I was that lucky baby. I was six months old. And I had just been left incapable of walking without support, for the rest of my life. Was I really 'lucky'? Yes, of course I was, I was alive, and all of the other babies were completely paralysed or dead.

I did not know then, and I don't know now, how my life might have developed and what I might have achieved without that damage to my nerves. But someone else's negligence changed my life forever.

When the parents of the affected babies realised that their children were deteriorating fast, they rushed to the hospital. They were horrified, scared, and very angry. They were asking, "What happened?" "Why did it happen?" "Why was my baby damaged?" "Why did my baby die?" Of course, they did not get any answers. Even to this day there are no answers.

The nurse was gone and the hospital authorities claimed that they had no idea of her identity or where she was at that moment or how she even got into the hospital. There was no investigation. It was no big deal. It was just another day in the life of a Romanian hospital in 1980.

Just like the other parents whose babies were paralysed or dead, my parents ran helplessly through the corridors of the hospital with me wrapped in a blanket. They asked one person after another the same question. "Can you tell us why our son's leg is hanging limp?". They went on to tell the story about the nurse, but no one really cared. My parents appeared shabby in their tattered clothes and old, worn-out shoes. No one took them seriously because they were poor people. Poor people were no more than puppets in the hands of the communist regime back then. Most people did not have any power or voice. There was no one in authority that was prepared to listen to poor people. My parents were just like most people in Romania: every day brought a new set of challenges, the biggest being survival. They did not have the luxury to dream or be ambitious. How could they think about tomorrow when they had to struggle to get through today?

The hospital authorities took their usual arrogant position, they accused my parents of making up the story to extract some money. Some said that my limp leg was not the result of a wrong injection but of a congenital deformity, and my parents had only observed it now. My parents still have photos of me before I had the injection – I was perfectly normal, I had both my legs functioning as they should.

My Mum and Dad kept coming back to the hospital every day in the hope of seeing that nurse again - but they never did. They kept coming back in the hope of finding someone who would tell them what had really happened, but no-one could. Even more importantly, they kept coming back in the desperate hope of finding someone who would tell them that I could be cured. But my parents' cries were silenced by people's indifference. That was the attitude of doctors and nurses then – unfortunately some of them in 21st century Romanian hospitals still have the same attitude.

My parents had limited resources - no decent formal education or means of income; my dad worked in the construction industry as a labourer and my mum, in a chocolate factory. After the paralysis struck, my parents moved to Negoi, my mum's village, so that members of her family could help to take care of me. They settled for jobs in a farm with a meagre income, saving as much as they could, in the hope of getting me cured. Their determination to save me from the possibility of using wheelchair or walking with crutches was incredible. They would not give up. They did everything they could and to the best of their abilities.

I don't really remember much else from the time we moved to Negoi, until one day when my dad was told by a neighbor, in our village, that a certain doctor in the city of Craiova could help me. My parents had been told this so many times before, by so many other people: "He can cure your son", and they had been disappointed every single time.

But no matter how many doctors had failed them before, they were always full of hope that the next doctor would be able to cure me. Hope, however dim, seemed more comforting than accepting the fact that I, their son, would never be able to walk unattended. And so, they set out again. They went with renewed vigour and lots of hope and six months' worth of savings in a bundle, bound together by a rubber band. They were expecting to set things right.

My parents did not know the doctor's address. And they did not even know his full name. But it did not seem to be much of a concern for the trusting and hopeful people that my parents are. They took me from one person to another seeking directions and everyone seemed to know the answer. Everyone knew the address of the doctor we were looking for. Every answer sounded equally convincing. Yet, every door resulted in disappointment. They spent hours walking the streets of Craiova. Every wrong door took away a little bit of their hope, until none was left. Then, the tears flowed.

My dad held me tighter, pulling me closer towards his chest as he cried, his arms wrapped around me in a protective embrace. I could hear his heart beating loudly and feel his body shivering. My mum kept running her hands through my hair and saying, "We love you Vas" between sobs. My parents sat on the steps outside a church, tired and completely shattered.

The beads of sweat on my dad's forehead and heavy breathing told a familiar tale. My dad and mum had travelled all the way from our village to the city of Craiova in Romania, to seek a remedy for my illness, to cure my disability. My dad, carrying me in his arms, along with my mum, had been knocking on doors of every church and hospital the entire day. I think I must have been 4-5 years old at the time. I can't really remember exactly my age, but I do remember this particular day very well.

I look back at this distant memory and wonder what really made them cry. Were they frustrated because no one could guide us to the path, the end of which, my parents could see so clearly? Or was the realization finally sinking in that it was all over and they needed to accept the truth that I would never walk? The crutches, or a wheelchair, were going to be my reality and they could do nothing but live with it. I suppose they felt guilty and responsible for what had happened.

My parents' tears moved something deep inside me. I felt their pain and hurt. As a 4-5 year old, I could not fully understand the reason behind the tears and the hugs and gentle words, but it deeply affected me nevertheless.

For a child, parents are super heroes. They are the superstars who protect them from all that is evil. They are the A team who cannot be broken down by anything that the world throws at them. But, in that moment of desperation I remember that my parents broke down: their super-strength was disappearing and they were showing their helpless side. It was something that I had never seen before. And I knew that I never wanted to see them that way ever again. So, I decided that I would never let my parents feel defeated and hopeless ever again because of the fact that I could not walk like a normal person. Looking back, I realize that it was one of the most defining moments of my life. I had found a reason to fight and never give up. I had found a reason to strive.

Chapter 2

My First Birthday Present: A Pair of Crutches

*"Thank you' is the best prayer that anyone could say. I say that one a lot. Thank you expresses extreme gratitude, humility, understanding." - **Alice Walker***

On my fifth birthday, Uncle Costin came to visit us. I could see that he had a pair of long wooden frames with him. I had no idea what they were. He picked me up and took me outside our house and handed them over to me, "Happy birthday Vasi!". I was really happy to get a birthday present. I had never received one before. And even though I had no idea what to do with them, I was still quite excited.

He put me down and helped me stand up with their support by tucking them under my arms. "These are crutches Vasi, and they are going to help you walk", Uncle Costin said. I was thrilled. I was going to walk just like everyone else, and couldn't wait to start playing football. With my parents, brother and sisters cheering me on, with Uncle Costin's help, I took my first step. Everything around me felt so different. It was a very different view to the one I had before, while crawling around.

Everything and everyone seemed a little less big than they used to. I felt like a giant, but I also felt that I was equal to everyone else now. People would not look down at me, and I was not looking up at them, unless they were much taller than myself – most of them were, but I was standing up on my own foot! Life seemed very promising at that time.

Although grateful and excited at first, I found it extremely painful as the days passed by. I kept falling and hurting myself. My armpits, shoulders and palms used to get so sore that I just wanted to throw the crutches away and crawl about as I did before. But my mum and dad convinced me that things would get better in a few days and the pain would gradually decline. So I kept trying. And even though it did not get any less painful, things did get better in a lot of ways. And I learned to accept the pain as a part of the process.

Climbing Trees

"Vas! What are you doing? You will fall!", my mum shouted as she came running towards me. I was trying to climb the apple tree just beyond the fence, right outside our house. Again. I was five years old. Everything seemed extraordinary and wonderful back then. Especially the trees.

A week before, I had sat under the very tree in my favourite spot and soaked in the sun as it filtered through the vivid red leaves; all of a sudden, my gaze had fallen on a branch way up high, I could see a nest but it seemed empty. I needed to find out.

I had tried to climb the tree every day since that beautiful summer morning. I had landed on the ground every single time with bruised knees and palms. But today was not going to be just another day. I had made up my mind that this was not going to be another failed attempt.

I used to step outside our house every day after solemnly promising my mum that I would not do anything to hurt myself. And then I would forget all about it in the excitement of discovering something new and exciting. Even from a distance, I could tell that mum was furious. But I had a job to do so I continued climbing the tree.

I had already pulled myself up by holding on to the lowest branch and pushing my right foot against the ground. I then grabbed the next branch and continued climbing. By the time my mum got there, I was well beyond her reach and ignored her pleas completely.

I finally reached the nest and looked inside. It was empty. But far from being disappointed it seemed like the happiest moment of my life. I had just climbed a tree. The sun seemed within my reach. I looked down at my mum, horror spread across her face; I grinned and waved my hands to console her.

"Mum, I made it!", I yelled.

"Get down now before you fall down and hurt yourself!" she yelled back at me.

Chapter 3

Leaving Home at the age of 7

"Leaving home, in a sense, involves a kind of second birth in which we give birth to ourselves." - **Robert Neelly Bellah**

In 1987 Life took an unexpected turn when at the age of seven I was packed off to a boarding school in Jucu, Cluj-Napoca for disabled boys. My parents could not afford to send me to the normal school in our village, as they would have had to take me to school and pick me up. Their jobs stared at 4 am and they used to get home at 6pm. I was devastated when I heard that I would be leaving my parents, my brother, two sisters and my friends, and move 500km (over 300 miles) away. I didn't understand why my family wanted to send me to a school that was so far away from them – I felt abandoned. From the moment they turned their backs on me, left me there and returned home, I sort of disliked them. I thought I would never see them again even though they assured me that they would come to get me on school holidays; I didn't understand any of that. In my heart I wanted to know why they had left me there. Things did not make sense. I was very upset for a long time, until I realised why they had done that. I couldn't even concentrate in the classroom – I was constantly thinking of my family.

I no longer had my mum or my family to fall back on. When I was at home, my mum encouraged me to be as self-dependent as possible. But, I was still a seven-year-old and she cooked for me, made my bed and, very importantly, if I was having a bad day she could take it all away with a hug and a kiss. And suddenly, I had no one to run home to, when I got hurt.

At Jucu I had to make my bed, wash my clothes, clean the room and tidy the school grounds – a ritual followed by all the boys in the school. Getting bullied by older kids and completing their tasks was a part of the ritual too. We had to wake up at 6:30 in the morning and finish our chores by 8:00, before our lessons started. In sub-zero temperatures, this was much harder than it sounds. My hands used to shrivel up because of the cold water that we had to use. We only had hot water once a week – on a Friday. That's when we all rushed to have proper showers. It was like heaven to have hot water running on our bodies.

We used to witness very harsh winters most of the time, but one particular winter it was really bad. I can't exactly remember how old I was. My weak leg had started acting up again. Every year at home, the onset of winter meant that everyone paid extra attention to me. I discovered quite early that extremely low temperatures resulted in poor blood circulation in my weaker leg, causing a lot of discomfort. I would get a terrible, mind-numbing pain in my weak leg every year during winter. Warmth was the only cure, because medicines did not work. So my brother and sisters used to wrap up my leg in all the warm clothes they could possibly find around the house.

But things were different at the boarding school and I had to take care of myself. I was expected to carry out my responsibilities just like the others, irrespective of the pain I was in. There were no privileges here. I could not cry and throw a tantrum expecting everyone to drop everything and come to my aid, because no one would.

So, I continued cleaning the ground and doing all the chores, even though I was struggling to walk. I could not speak up because the older kids would have picked on me. Whatever the teachers might say, the unwritten rules were 1. If you are vulnerable, you are weak, and you are fair game to the bigger and stronger boys. 2. Keep your feelings to yourself because no-one has the time or wish to sort out your drama – they are too busy dealing with their own. If I was going to survive I would have to follow the rules like everyone else.

In just one week, the pain had become so unbearable that I could barely sleep. Since I did not have enough warm clothes with me, I used to wrap my leg in anything I could find, including the bed cover. Underneath my uniform, I used to tie a couple of handkerchiefs tightly around my leg to try to subdue the pain. And of course it did not work very well.

I continued this way until one day, I woke up and I could not feel my leg at all. I was absolutely terrified fearing the worst. I knew I could not pull it off anymore, so I told my teacher and a week's bed rest followed.

I was bullied for weeks after the incident. The older children called me names such as wimp, and picked on me. I also learnt that this was how it was going to be, always. There would be no privileges and the world would not wait for me to catch up. And if my disability was a weakness, I would have to find a way to deal with it. No one else would do it for me.

I was breathing heavily and with every breath, I was creating small specks of mist that looked like clouds; I gazed at them, almost in a trance, and I found myself looking at a familiar place. A boy was cleaning a vast field, trying hard to balance on his crutches. Shivering violently in the cold, and picking up scraps of garbage strewn across the ground, he cut a rather lonely figure, accompanied only by a thin mist that hung delicately a few feet above the grass. I was looking at myself, cleaning my school grounds...

I did not have a pair of gloves; an old torn jumper over a t-shirt was my only shield against the biting cold as I cleaned the ground. My hands had turned a sick shade of blue. My weak leg, as always, had been affected the most. The pain was unlike anything I had ever experienced before. I honestly thought that I was going to lose my leg and end up with a peg leg like a pirate! I just wished that I was snuggled up in my nice warm bed at home...

I looked at the supervising teacher; the layers of clothing on him could clothe my entire family. His hands tucked inside his blazer pockets, he was giving me a disapproving, stern look. I could not stand the pain anymore and decided to tell him that I needed to go back to my room. I mustered whatever was left in me and went to him, "I need to go back to my room, Sir", I said, and put up my blue palms to prove that I had a problem.

He looked at me with utter disgust and put his long cane to use. It did warm my hands but not in a good way. I cried out in agony. I looked straight into his eyes. I could see that he was rather pleased with himself. His cane was still raised, ready to strike again if needed. But I could not care less and I swore at him, loud and clear. As if the weather was not terrible enough, I had to put up with an idiot and his cane. I uttered a rich choice of words, without caring much about what he would do next.

And the cane struck a second time - sharper, louder and tearing into my flesh. Without giving a second thought about the consequences and ignoring his threats about complaining to the headmaster, I turned my back to him and hobbled my way back to the room.

Once I reached my room, I closed the door and wept bitterly. "Why did my parents abandon me like this?", I thought to myself. My anger, pain and frustration blinded me to the fact that this was for my own good. It was a dramatic change for me and life at home had never seemed so luxurious before. I missed my family terribly. I missed being a seven year old. I missed being a kid.

These sort of treatments from our teachers and supervises, at the bording school, were not uncommon. We used to be treated as if we were prisoners there. We only had one slice of bread for breakfast, two slices at lunchtime and one slice for dinner together with a cup of tea. If we wanted to leave the school grounds, to go into the village for shopping or for a non-alcoholic drink, we had to have a written note from the head master with three days in advance. Survival was our first priority. Strangely we felt happy – we used to organize football and table tennis competitions and we used to have a lot of fun. We really enjoyed ourselves at these games when the girls from the village used to come and watch us...it was then that we really put our best performance on, and forgot about the hardships.

Chapter 4

Struggling With People's Perceptions

"Disability is a matter of perception. If you can do just one thing well, you're needed by someone." - **Martina Navratilova**

When we make a mistake, we usually have to put up with the consequences. However much we hate the experience we have no-one but ourselves to blame for our own mistakes. But what do you do when you have to live with consequences of someone else's mistake? I was at the wrong place at the wrong time. The nurse who administered the wrong injection made a mistake. The hospital authorities who ignored my parents and refused to act quickly made a mistake. So, why did I have to suffer for the rest of my life? Why did they get away with their mistake? Why did this happen to me at such a young age? What did I do wrong? I could never answer these questions – and I still cannot answer them even to this day.

As a child, I did not struggle as much dealing with my condition, as I struggled with people's reactions when they found out that I had a disability. Strangers, neighbours, and sometimes, even my friends seemed to make a big fuss about the fact that I was not like them. It seemed to affect everyone else more than it affected me. I realized that, even though I lived with the problem of being physically disabled, there was a greater problem in the minds of those who failed to see past my crutches. Their way of thinking about my disability exhausted me.

People would ask me if I could do the things that they could, and if I said yes, they wondered how. Patiently I tried to answer all the questions that came my way but given a choice, I preferred to be like any other boy who could just live his life without any unnecessary drama, instead of being constantly interviewed. I found my escape from all these questions in sports, and my greatest joy came from playing football.

Even when I was very young, whenever someone asked me what I wanted to be when I grew up, I would promptly respond, "a footballer!", much to the amusement of the person in front of me, sizing me up, eyeing the pair of crutches, sometimes with dismay, often with pity. However, nothing ever came in my way of seeing this glorious dream turn into reality night after night in my sleep. I was certain that I would be cured in no time and become a professional footballer, just like the ones I watched playing in the football stadium, near my home in Romania.

I spent a great deal of my childhood in the stadium, hopping around on my crutches, trying to tackle the football, with my brother or sometimes even alone. When I wanted to play with other kids none of them ever picked me to play on their team. I used to wonder why I was being treated like an outcast. When I asked them the same question, they would tell me, "You can't play with us because you won't be able to". I had no idea what they meant by that because I was perfectly capable of playing football just like them. Years later, it dawned on me that people did not usually identify a person with a bad leg as a footballer. My disability did not give people much confidence about what I could do.

I would often end up playing by myself while the rest of the kids played together just a short way away. They seemed to have such an amazing time playing together, and I really wanted to play with them. I wanted them to pick me first when the teams were being formed. The best ones were always picked first. I wanted them to know that I was really good. I needed one chance to prove myself, and I would do anything to get that chance.

So, one day, I bought a new football. If they wanted the football to play with, they would obviously have to pick me to play. "The kid with the ball calls the shots" - that is the unwritten rule that every child follows all over the world. Thus, I found my way in. I proved myself to be a decent player and I was never left out after that day, even when I did not have my football.

I still remember the first goal I scored while playing with the rest of the kids in the local park, I remember the surprised looks and all the attention I got afterwards. There was a slight drizzle that day while we were playing and twenty minutes into the game, I realized that no one from my team was passing the ball to me. I kept hopping around yelling at my team mates: "Over here, come on pass it here." But everyone ignored me. Looking back, I expect that they thought that I could not do anything with the ball, even if they did pass it to me. Of course, I did not realize this back then. I just thought that they could not hear me.

But I still got my chance when one of my team mates missed a pass. I kicked the ball right past the goalkeeper. Everyone from my team came running towards me. "So you can play", one of them said and I replied, "Yeah, that is what it looks like".

As a kid, I never thought that there was anything wrong with me. The way life appeared to me back then, it was normal and perfect. But everyone seemed to disagree and I could not understand why. Back in Romania, I was once asked, "What is wrong with you? Did you upset God?". It seemed that people had endless questions about my disability. I could not answer them – but still they kept coming.

That was when I started questioning. What were all these people seeing so clearly that I could not? Was there really something terribly wrong with me? Everyone seemed to wonder why I could not walk like them. The other kids would tell me that I could not play with them because their parents had told them not to.

"What is wrong with me mum?", I asked my mother one day after coming home. And she said, "You had an injection which damaged the nerves to the muscles of your leg. So you cannot walk like others". Even though she sounded perfectly calm, the agony in her eyes was hard to miss. I did not ask her any more questions.

After that day, I became aware that I was different. I was suddenly aware of the looks that I got from people. I understood what sympathy looked like. And more importantly, what it felt like. It felt painful. The world had convinced me that there was something wrong with me; I was not just different in their eyes, I was a mistake. I thought that way for a long time.

For a very long time, I struggled to understand why I could not lead a regular life just like my friends. The awkward glances and the piteous looks hurt me immensely. And all I could wish for, was to be just another face in the crowd.

But life, eventually, taught me the greatest lesson I have ever learnt. It is this: Not being normal is a privilege, it is a unique gift that only some have. Embrace the gift of not being what everyone else is. Embrace it because it will help you to be so much more than what everyone expects you to be. Embrace the fact that you are special. Embrace the fact that you are unique.

I did not have an answer back then but I do now. So if someone were to ask me those questions again, "What is wrong with you? Did you upset God?", I would say, "My design was changed for experimental purposes. Turns out, I did ok".

Chapter 5

My First Toy

"It is not how much we have, but how much we enjoy, that makes happiness." - **Charles Spurgeon**

I have two sisters and a brother, and all of us used to eagerly wait for Christmas every year. It meant to us what it means to so many other children - happiness and joy that comes wrapped in shiny paper and ribbons. But for us, it meant just a little more. Because it was the only time during the entire year that we got presents or anything new at all. And only if we were lucky enough and mum's and dad's savings had not been spent in an emergency. As mum put it, "Santa got caught up in some work, but he will make it up next year".

I was five years old, and my brother and I had been counting down the days until Christmas Eve. We had helped dad set up the Christmas tree with whatever little we had - tattered old decorations, broken pieces of tinsel, and lights. But what we put on that tree did not matter because it took the form we wanted to see. And it was the most beautiful thing we had ever set our eyes on.

We were really eager and excited about the presents we were going to get because "We had been on our best behaviour and Santa would surely get us something nice", mum had promised. My brother and I woke up to a flurry of snowflakes outside our window. It was Christmas Day! We were still rubbing our eyes when mum came into the room and said, "Santa has left gifts under the Christmas tree for both of you!".

I don't think I will ever be able to express the joy of seeing that bright red and yellow truck for the first time. As a child, at that moment, I was convinced that life could not get any better and I had the most precious thing in the world in my hands. I remember thinking to myself, "Mum and dad must be very rich!". It was my very first toy and the only one I had for the next two years. And every morning, for those two years, I woke up to look at it with the same fascinated look as I did the very first time.

Going After What You Want

As kids, my brother, sisters and I did not have many toys. We were fortunate enough to have a roof above our heads and three square meals a day. Everything else was a bonus. We did not make many demands on our parents because we knew how hard it was for them to provide for us. Except for one time that I remember quite distinctly.

My mum and I were waiting at the railway station; I was supposed to board the train that would take me to my boarding school in Cluj -Napoca. With an hour to go before the train's arrival, we decided to go for a stroll. As we walked around the railway station, a little shop caught my eye – it was stocked with a lot of sweets. For a ten-year-old it was like a magnet, drawing me closer.

I dragged my mum towards the shop but I could sense that she was not too keen. "Mum, let's go!", but she just stood in her place. I broke my hand free from her grip and walked towards the shop, leaving her behind. I stood there transfixed, eyeing a bar of chocolate in a beautiful red wrapper. I turned towards my mum who was still standing in the place where I had left her, looking at me. "Vas, the train will be here any moment now, come!", she said. I looked up at the clock and we still had half an hour more. "But look mum", I pointed upwards towards the clock, trying to tell her that we still had some time.

She still stood there, rummaging in her purse. I marched up to her and dragged her to the shop this time. Then I drew her attention to the chocolate that I wanted to buy. And I begged her to buy it for me. She refused but I was in a daze and my mind was in no state to accept refusal. So I asked her again, "Mum, please! Just this once". And she said, "Vas, I do not have any money, I used it all for the train ticket." My mind conveniently overlooked the guilt and misery in her eyes and focused on the task at hand. I started crying. I wanted that chocolate at any cost and nothing else mattered, not even the fact that my mum was utterly helpless.

As far as I can remember, it was the only time I ever made a demand of any kind and threw a fit.

Chapter 6

Being Treated As An Outsider

"I like the condition of being an outsider, just passing through." -
Barry Unsworth

I was eight years old, sitting outside our house, playing by myself when a group of three boys came by and started laughing at me. They aske3d each other what would happen if they kicked me really hard and ran away. Would I just sit there and cry, because I would not be able to do anything as I was disabled and could not run after them. While they were taunting me, they kept hitting me on the head with sticks. They were right, I could really not do anything if they decided to kick me, all I could do was sit and stare. "Leave me alone!", I yelled.

But they continued bullying me. I was getting really angry. I felt annoyed because I really was at their mercy. Why couldn't they leave me alone? I had done nothing to provoke them. Why were they being so mean? I grabbed my crutches and promised myself that I would give them back as good as I got without any intention of hurting them, but with the intention of showing them what it was like to be hit.

One of them came really close to me with the intention of hitting me and I swung my crutch at him with all my might right on the knee. Smack! His knee sounded like a twig making a sickening sound. I wasn't sure if I had broken it, but I acted like it wasn't a big deal. Later on when he couldn't move so quickly I realised that I actually hurt him. I was certain that he had got what he deserved even though I felt really bad about it. I felt really sorry, especially when he complained about the pain. Later that afternoon his grandmother came to our house to have a go at me because I had bruised his knee quite badly. I told her what they did to me, and that I was sorry about what I did. In the end she agreed that her grandson should not have taunted me, and she went home. After that incident I became very good friends with all three of the boys – even to this day we still meet up when I go back home, and we talk about that incident now. Even though it was not funny at the time, we are old enough to laugh about it now.

A similar incident occurred when I was ten; a boy threw a stone at me and called me names. It was absolutely uncalled for. He kept bullying me, ignoring my shouts to go away. I had had enough of it. I threw a branch at him. It hit him straight between the eyes and he bled a little bit. Fortunately, I did not cause any serious injury to him. Again, with this guy I became good friends afterwards.

There were only so many legs I could bruise, or heads I could cut. I could not go on being violent every time someone bullied me or called me names. My mum's words of support came to my rescue every single time. I learned from her to ignore the bullies. It is the greatest skill I have acquired, and the hardest. It is tough to be challenged for the way you are and not to feel bad. When you are hurt by the things that people say and do, it is easy to get hurt inside, and it is easy to do things designed to hurt these people. It is in our nature to defend what we stand for; the trick is in doing it in a way that you shout out without speaking a word, or breaking a bone. The trick is to let your deeds speak for the person you are.

I still get agitated when someone looks down on me because of my crutches. And sometimes, I really am tempted to pick something up and fling it really hard at the idiot, but I don't. Lowering myself to the level of the bully solves nothing. It does not make him better, and it make me feel worse.

When I was growing up I never went hungry at home. My parents always managed to put food on the table. I was like any other boy who loved sports, the outdoors and wore his wounds like a badge of honour. I have had my fair share of misses though. I did not get a chance to enjoy my childhood as much as I would have wanted to. I had to toughen up quite early in life; I had to get used to the constant dismay and disapproval by the people around me, especially the girls of my age who always made fun of me and thought that I was good for nothing. I spent most of my time being treated like an outsider by the other kids.

My mum once told me "There will be a lot of times when people won't understand you and they will disrespect you for how you are. But don't let that stop you from doing what you want to do. If they are wise, they will reach out to you. If they are not, then that is their problem, not yours. It will take time for people to understand you because you are not like them. Just be patient".

As a child, once I became aware that I was treated differently because of how I walked, I started trying to walk like my friends, using both legs, without my crutches. I was quite convinced that if I tried hard enough, I could do it. I used to wrap my arms around the shoulders of friends, one on either side and tried to walk like them.

Right foot, then left foot, ouch! The very first time I tried walking normally, I thought that my left leg would just collapse under the weight of my body. And even though my friends, Tavi and Raul, were helping me, I could only take a few steps on my first attempt. It was way too painful. But I kept trying, hoping that it would get easier. It never did. And I gave up. I eventually realized that I did not need to walk like others. Especially when I did such a tremendous job of walking like myself!

Over the years, I realized that there were some important skills that I needed to master – adaptation and improvisation. I learned to swim by paddling with one leg. I learned to play table-tennis while hopping around on one leg and one crutch. The great reward for me was that these adaptations worked for me. I won prizes for swimming and for table-tennis. I adapted instead of wasting my time trying to figure why I could not do things the way everyone else did. The way I saw it, I was redefining what normal meant for me – and what normal meant for everyone else!

Chapter 7

Boarding the Wrong Train

*"Don't be afraid to take unfamiliar paths, sometimes they are the ones that take you to the best places." - **Unknown***

It was sports day in our school and I had left home that morning early, really thrilled at the prospect of taking part in a race. "Mum, I am going to get the first prize!", I told my mother excitedly. And she said, "I want you to finish that race because that is all that matters, it does not matter whether you win or lose". I did not quite understand but nodded my head. What could be more important than winning?

A lot of my friends had already put in their names and I went eagerly to give my name too. But my sports teacher simply refused, "You cannot take part. Go and watch your friends run, cheer for them". "Why not? Why can't I take part in the race", I asked. And she said, "Because you can't".

She refused to change her mind but fortunately, one of my teachers who really supported me, convinced her to add my name and she finally did.

There were ten of us at the starting line waiting for the race to begin. I was on all fours. "On your marks, get set, go!". We all started running and all my friends raced ahead of me. I tried so hard to catch up but I could not. And by the time one of my friends crossed the finish line, I had barely completed half the race and I knew then, that I would finish last. But I remembered what my mum had said, "...finish that race because that is all that matters". And I did.

I may not win the race, but I will make it to the finish line, no matter what.

It reminded me of the time when I was heading back to my boarding school in Jucu, Cluj-Napoca after summer vacations. I had endured an exhausting seven hours journey to reach the railway station from where I was supposed to board the train.

I went to the usual platform from where the train always left and boarded the one going in the opposite direction. I was hardly conscious as the long journey had completely drained me. I was all set for a quick nap. Barely five minutes into the journey, and moments away from falling asleep, I realized that something was not quite right. I could hear my co-passengers talking amongst themselves, their conversations hardly audible over the sounds of the train moving along the railway line. I was extremely sleepy and I could not really figure out what they were saying but something seemed odd...why were they all mentioning places that did not fall on the route?

I looked outside the window and even though it was dark, I could figure that this was not the same familiar route that the train always took on the way to my school. The buildings were not the ones that always greeted me on my way. The roads were not lighted; my usual train route was parallel to a motorway that had lights and no matter what time of the day, one could always see the never-ending stream of traffic, hooting each other, the fast ones overtaking the slow ones, and all against a background of noise. It hit me that I had boarded the wrong train and suddenly, I was not feeling so sleepy anymore.

I felt alarmed and my throat went dry; "You boarded the wrong train!", my mind kept yelling at me over and over again. I was so angry with myself for having made such a silly mistake. This was not a familiar place and it was making me extremely uncomfortable. I was scared. Where was I going? What would I do in a strange town? How would I get to school? Would I ever see my family and friends again? H-E-L-P!! I was already thinking of ghastly scenarios all of which ended in tragedy.

I was not in a familiar place and it was scary. I didn't know the place and the people. What would I do if something went wrong? Change threatens us because it makes us an alien in strange surroundings. Change is scary because we are no longer in control. But change is also good, it might not be comfortable, but it is good – it makes us move outside our comfort zone, and once beyond that, we can be unstoppable!

I looked outside the window; it was a strange and an almost haunting sight, intimidating and unfamiliar. Whilst the train was moving slowly, and as my vision adjusted to the darkness, I realized that the place was swarming with activity, perhaps more than what I usually witnessed on my usual route. People were walking around, rushing to their destinations. The more I realized that this place was not very different from my familiar route, the calmer I felt. I started thinking rationally. I could get out at the next station and board another train. In the meantime, I could just sit back and enjoy the ride. It was not so bad after all. It was like an adventure.

It would make perfect sense if I hated the nurse, but I never did. Why? Just like boarding the wrong train made me discover a new place, and gave me a unique experience which I would have otherwise missed if I had taken the usual route, so her mistake changed the direction in which my life was headed. And just like it was hard for me to initially overcome the paralyzing fear of being in a situation that I never expected as I headed in the wrong direction on a train, my life has been a rough ride too. I have been lost and scared in the darkness that seemed to cast a shadow over my life but eventually, I taught myself to see the light, and enjoy my life for what it is. I never hated the nurse because she got me on the 'wrong train' and I have absolutely loved the ride!

So, next time you find yourself going in the wrong direction, don't let panic take over. Don't let panic trick you into thinking that disaster is waiting for you around the corner. Take a deep breath. Remember that you have a way of escape. Look around you and realise that you have the power in your own hands to take control of your life. Sometimes it is necessary to lose control just to remind yourself that you can grab it back again if you choose to do so.

Chapter 8

Unanswered Questions

*"Your job is not to answer; your job is to ask. The answer will come to you." - **Vasile Onica***

I was 12 years old. One winter afternoon in Jucu, three of my classmates and I decided to go to the park behind our boarding school. The sledge at the top of the hill looked rather inviting and my friend and I mounted it. We screamed with delight all the way down. But I continued screaming even after we had reached the bottom of the hill. We had rammed straight into a tree and it had broken my right leg.

"As you can see in the x-ray, the tibia of your right leg is fractured. It will have to stay in a plaster for 6-8 weeks", the doctor said. "There goes my holiday", I thought to myself.

My mum came the next day to pick me up and take me home with her for the holiday. And that is exactly what she did. She carried me in her arms to the railway station, while getting on the train, at the bus-stop, in the bus, all the way to home. And not once did she complain or yell at me.

Once we were home, my brother and sisters gladly took on the responsibility of taking care of me. My brother used to carry me over his back all around the house and even to the stadium to watch other boys playing football. They were all happy to have me around, fractured leg or not; it did not make any difference to them.

A lot of things changed in the years that followed, including me, but one thing remained a constant - my dream of becoming a footballer. It turned into an obsession as I thought about it day in and day out. I used to imagine that I would be cured somehow, that I would go on to become a professional footballer, and I would get to represent my country in the national football team. I imagined myself playing in large stadiums in front of huge crowds, cheering me on. I used to play football for several hours in the school playground knowing with absolute certainty that I would be playing in a much larger playground someday.

I sometimes asked myself questions such as: Why was I not allowed to follow my childhood dream? Why was I given that injection? What did I do wrong to deserve this? Why me? Would life really have steered me on to become a professional footballer?

I could never answer these questions and I realized that there was no point in trying to find those answers. I just knew one thing - I had a choice. I could forgive and move on, and face whatever was in store for me, or I could carry the hurt and the pain of being wronged by someone and let it infect my thoughts and existence. I chose to forgive because the choice not to, would have come at a greater cost. I could have let the mistake of that stranger destroy me; I let it define me instead. At the age of 14 years I started to be grateful for my life as it was, and for the mistake which that nurse had made that left me on crutches for the rest of my life. Once I started to be grateful for the way I was and for what I had in my life, things started to improve for me; I was much happier, I had a lot more friends, and the things I wanted to do, or have, seemed to come my way without any big effort.

I never got to the point of hating the nurse because I had no reason to. She gave me a life worth fighting for. Had I not been on crutches, I would never have been judged so harshly by people. Had I never been questioned repeatedly, I would never have tried so hard to seek the answers. Had I never been challenged so hard, I would not have tried so hard to overcome those challenges. I discovered myself because I got lost. So, I thanked her instead. And I wished her well.

PART 2

MOVING TO THE UK

Chapter 9

An Opportunity Presented Itself

*"One secret of success in life is for a man to be ready for his opportunity when it comes." - **Benjamin Disraeli***

I was in my boarding school when my foster father, Dr Stuart Newton visited our school for the first time in 1990. He had come to Jucu with a group of students from his school in London. But it was not until 1992 that I got a chance to meet him...

I was playing football in the school playground with some of my friends on a Saturday afternoon, when I was summoned by our headmaster. I thought that I was in some serious trouble. The moment I walked into the office, our headmaster introduced me to Dr Newton and asked me a simple question, "How would you like to go to England?" I did not think twice before saying, "Yes! I would love to", even though I had no idea why my headmaster suddenly wished to know whether I would want to go to another country. I was soon dismissed without any further clarification. Not that I needed any, I had more important things to do, I had a football game to go back to.

Several days passed after this incident, and I soon forgot about it. Until I was summoned again to the headmaster's office one day, who then informed me that I would be going to England with Dr Newton to seek medical advice from doctors about my leg. Fireworks went off in my head instantly. I felt like my prayers were going to be answered finally.

However, all this was not going to be so easy. I was not going to have my prayers answered overnight. It took two long years to get through the formalities. During this time, I continued my schooling while my parents and the school authorities took care of the paperwork such as creating a personal I.D. for my passport. My parents had to travel back and forth from Negoi, in southern Romania, where we lived to my school, and then to Bucharest to sign the necessary papers giving their consent that I could travel to England with Dr Newton. Even though it was a very long process, I was absolutely certain that I would be in England by the end of it.

Finally, in July 1994, during vacations, I was scheduled to leave for England. I was at the boarding school, waiting for Dr Newton to arrive. I had been told that he would arrive in the morning. I waited till late evening, but he did not turn up. I convinced myself that there must have been some problem and he would be there for me on the second day. I was quite hopeful. I had waited for two years for this day, I could certainly wait for a day more. But it was the same story on the second day too. By the third day, I was beginning to have doubts about everything; a friend of mine had told me a week before that it was too good to be true. Maybe, he was right. A part of me was thinking about going back home but I decided to stay back for another day.

The next day, I got the news that Dr Newton would be coming on Monday. There had been a miscommunication between the school authorities and Dr Newton. I was thrilled beyond measure. And my faith was restored.

Monday morning, I got up early, got dressed, wore my best clothes and my widest smile. I just kept thinking about the events that were going to unfold in the next few days. The moment I saw Dr Newton entering the school gates, I pinched myself to make sure that I was not dreaming. I felt really happy and hopeful when I saw him.

The next day, we were off to Bucharest in an overnight train. I barely got any sleep that night, part of it came from the excitement of going to a completely new place, and the rest, from how my life was going to change after this adventure.

The taxi ride from Gara de Nord train station, in Bucharest, to Otopeni airport was absolutely magical. To any other person, it may have been just another morning but for me, the warmth of the sun, the blue sky, the birds singing were all positive signs that my life was changing forever and that wonderful things were waiting for me. I was full of optimism and happiness.

My first time in an airplane was just as magical. As I saw the clouds drifting past below my window while we were flying up high, I felt like it was just the beginning of all the beautiful things life had in store for me. I felt an assurance that things were going to get better.

Once we reached UK, and the moment I stepped into the airport, I experienced a remarkable difference in people's attitudes towards me. No one was staring at me. I was just another face in the crowd. I did not get any weird looks like I always did back home.

The next six weeks that I spent with Dr Newton's family were absolutely wonderful. People were extremely friendly, and no one ever looked at me like I was some freak of nature. It was so great to be treated just like any other normal boy – just the way I thought I was.

Even though I was having a great time there, my parents were worried sick about me. I kept getting letters from my mum, who sounded very anxious about my well-being. She was worried that I would never come back. She was also worried that if something happened to me, she would not be around to take care of me. I remember writing back to her, assuring her that I was going to be fine and back home in a few weeks, but my words were not enough to console her.

It was only after I returned home after six weeks that my mum finally relaxed. Once my parents learnt about how I was treated in UK by Dr Newton's family and people in general, they felt that I should perhaps move to UK as I would have a lot more opportunities there.

I got back to my usual life in my boarding school after this little adventure. In the meantime, my parents, the school authorities and Dr Newton, were again setting things up to send me to England the next year.

In 1995, I went to UK again for a period of 6 weeks. I had been told that Dr Newton would be taking me to a specialist for treating my leg. Aboard the flight, all the way from Bucharest to London, I was thinking about what the future held for me – in a week's time, I would be able to walk again. I would go on to realize my dream of becoming a footballer. I would be playing in a stadium cheered on by thousands of people. I could barely contain the excitement.

No one had told me that I was going to walk again. I had simply told myself that story because I really wanted to believe that I was going to get better.

In UK, Dr Newton took me to a specialist who made it clear that the surgery would not help me walk without crutches again. It would barely ease some of the discomfort I experienced in my leg during harsh weather. But I was too caught up in my dream of becoming a footballer. And it was convenient to look away from reality in order to believe that my dream would come true. I was absolutely convinced that I was going to return home without my crutches.

But I learnt that this was not going to be simple. It would take a long time to make this happen. It took two more years. Since I was still a minor at that time, there were a lot of formalities that had to be gone through before the surgery could be performed in UK; the doctor's report had to be legally translated into Romanian which was then handed over to doctors in Romania who briefed my parents accordingly. The doctors in UK then had to write a letter to the British embassy in Romania explaining my need for a medical visa. A lot of documents were mailed back and forth between my parents and my boarding school in Romania to Dr Newton in England.

While all of this was going on, I returned to my school in Jucu, Cluj-Napoca, holding on to the hope of a better future. Now that I look back, I realize that everyone around me knew that the surgery would not change my life drastically but somehow I had convinced myself otherwise. I patiently waited for everything to fall into place.

Chapter 10

A Crushed Dream

"When one dream dies, dream another dream." -

Vasile Onica

I flew back to England at the beginning of August 1997 for my surgery. I still remember the date so vividly - 4th of August. As I was being taken into the operating theatre, on the 8th of August, I kept thinking about my parents back home. They had not been able to come with me because they could not afford to, but I was certain that I was in their prayers at that precise moment. I was imagining the looks on their faces when they saw me again, standing on my legs, without the crutches. I could see the smile on my mother's face so clearly and I could see the pride in her eyes. My dad, my brother and my sisters, they would all be so happy. All the sacrifices that they had made all these years, all the pain that they had suffered in silence, it would all go away in that precious moment. Now that I look back, I realize that I was in a world of my own creation, weaving fantasies and dreams that were doomed from the beginning.

I snapped out of my thoughts as I was being given anaesthetics, and as I lost consciousness, I remember my last thought being, "When I wake up, my life will have changed, I will be able to walk without the crutches".

I woke up several hours later, groggy and utterly confused. I looked at my leg, and then, around the room for someone, anyone who could tell me what had happened. There was a nurse standing nearby who then called the doctors. I knew from the look on their faces that nothing had changed.

Once they started talking, I realized that my dream of being able to walk was indeed over. Yet, somewhere at the back of my mind, I kept telling myself that they were joking. Any moment they would start laughing and tell me that the operation was a huge success and I was going to walk out of the hospital room without my crutches. It was a cruel joke but I would forgive them. Any moment now, they were going to say that it was a joke...but the moment never came. I could not hear their kind words. I could not feel anything at all. Soon, everybody left.

I lay on the hospital bed for a long time. I just felt numb. I could not think or grieve. I could hear the loud tick-tock of the clock in my room, every other sound had just died. Several minutes passed, or maybe more, and then out of the blue, a surge of emotions hit me like a tidal wave, submerging me; I kept struggling, trying to come up for air but it kept me underneath until I knew that my dream of becoming a footballer would remain just that, a dream.

My dream had been completely torn apart, years of hope and optimism all wasted in just one moment. For the first time in my life, the reality of my existence sank in and it broke me down completely.

I had, until that point in my life, held an unwavering belief that things were going to be fine and I was going to be just like any other boy my age. A life without crutches seemed like a wonderful idea. I looked at my friends who did not have any disability, and they seemed to have a great life. They did not have to bear awkward glances from other people or struggle to accomplish everyday activities like climbing stairs. Unlike me, they did not have to constantly answer pointless questions and then justify those answers.

I wanted a similar life - a normal, regular life. I had held on to that dream for as long as I could remember. And now, I was watching it break apart in front of my eyes. Even though I worked really hard to never let my disability become an excuse for not achieving or doing everything that all of my friends could, I knew that, beyond a certain point, there were things that other people could do, and I just could not do. I had, long ago, worked out that I could not become a professional footballer if I walked with crutches. Now I understood that I would always have to walk with crutches. Now I understood that I could NEVER become a professional footballer.

I looked at my stitched up limp leg, tattered and weak. The scars from the operation had been covered by a lot of bandages but what about the state of my mind? They could not cover up those scars with any amount of bandages. The wounds just sat there, raw and painful. Then, I cried my heart out.

In that hospital in London, August 1997, at the age of 17, I felt like an alien. Strangers surrounded me, and I was far away from my home and family. How could I let my emotions show? Yet, all I wanted to do was to grieve. I did not want to pretend that I was not affected. I did not want to act tough. I did not have anything left in me to hide the way I felt – weak and helpless. I wished that my mum was there because she would have just let me be and only she could truly understand how I felt. But there was someone else.

Amongst all the unfamiliar faces, Dr Newton's was the only one that seemed genuinely affected by what I was going through. There was a kindness in his eyes that soothed me. So when he reached out to me, I responded.

Grief is a powerful emotion. It helps us let go of the misery that threatens to drown us after we have had a bad experience. It is alright to shed a few tears. But often, we can get stuck in one place, grieving and refusing to move ahead with our lives. Because in that moment, we feel that we are facing the absolute worst phase of our lives.

My life has taught me some powerful lessons. One of the most important is this: however good today is, there will be even better days in the future, AND however bad today is, there will be worse things that you have to face in the future. So use every experience you have, good or bad, to learn and to prepare yourself for what your future holds. If you have a terrible experience, express your disappointment and hurt, shed a few tears, but most importantly, wipe those tears away, learn your lesson and move ahead with your life as a stronger person who can now face even harsher circumstances – and overcome them with a lot more ease.

I was utterly miserable because the dream that I had seen from my childhood days right through my teenage years had just shattered. It was very difficult for me to make peace with the fact that I needed to put this chapter of my life behind me. I felt this horrible, hollow feeling inside me. I just did not want to go on but I eventually decided to find my way out because that was the only way to move ahead in my life, to face greater challenges and joys. I could not just sit there grieving, and expect my life to get better.

So I chose not to be depressed. It was pathetic enough that so many people pitied me because of my disability, I was not going to just sit there and pity myself. I told myself over and over again, that something good was in store for me in the future; I had perhaps, a role to play in the greater scheme of things. I told myself that if I cannot become a footballer, maybe, there is something better in store for me.

The hope of a better future was the only thing that kept me going. I knew it was my best bet to survive. In fact, hope was my only bet to survive. I could not move ahead in my life if I believed that I was going to face a dark future. I had to believe that my life was going to get better. And that is exactly what I did, I honestly believed that I had yet to see the best that my life had to offer.

The cure of a broken dream was much simpler; I saw a bigger and better dream – I promised myself that I would own a football club sometime in the future! It may sound ridiculous, but that is the very nature of dreams. Dreams often seem too strange to everyone else. But who cares if everyone else thinks that they are strange? Your dreams are personal, they are part of you. If other people laugh at them, that's their problem. The day will come when you will be the one laughing – make sure of that!

Someday, there will be another boy like me, hopping around on crutches, in the rain, trying to tackle a football, wanting to become a football player, stars in his eyes, trying to fight the odds and making sense of a world that is modelled by people who do not have to walk with crutches. May be on that day, I will be able to help that boy achieve his dreams and perhaps then, I will be able to find my place in the bigger scheme of things. Until that time, I will dream of climbing mountains.

Chapter 11

Life after the Operation

*"People are anxious to improve their circumstances, but are unwilling to improve themselves. That is why they remain bound." - **James Allen***

After the operation I was in the hospital for one week, during which time I was slowly struggling to accept the fact that I would never become a professional footballer or walk like a normal person.

My last thought before going into the operating theatre had been, "When I wake up, my life will have changed, I will be able to walk without the crutches". I realized years later, that my life had indeed changed post surgery. It hurt at that moment because the change I had hoped for, was not the change that occurred. Had the outcome of the surgery been what I was hoping for, I would have been able to walk. And I would have realised my childhood dream of becoming a footballer. Everything in my life would have been simplified. But none of those things happened.

People in the hospital (St. Thomas) were amazing, they tried to help me forget that I was never going to walk properly. Everyone, especially the nurses, used to come and play games (chess mainly) with me, and bring me sweets. But there was one particular lady doctor who was very special to me, her name was Dr. Haissam. She had an amazing smile, and a great heart. I could not understand much English then, but I could feel how genuine she was. On her time off, she used to come to visit me, and play chess with me. Those were my best memories in the hospital. I guess it helped that she was very beautiful too! At that age I wasn't into girls that much, especially after realizing that I would never be able to walk using both my legs, but Dr Haissam really impressed me. I really liked her. One day I got my Romanian-English dictionary out, and before she was due to arrive, I put together five words sentence; "you have a beautiful smile" and told her when she got there. From what I remember she blushed a little, and then she told me: "you are a very special young man, Vas" – that made me smile, and made my life in the hospital easier. From then on I found it much easier to convince myself that things were going to be good even though I could not walk using both legs, but I was still grieving every time I used to think that I would never be able to become a footballer – that really affected me badly.

In August 1997, after a week in the hospital, I came home to Dr Newton's family and I was looked after extremely well. I used to talk to my foster father about football, and life. We also used to talk about the beautiful lady doctor.

After the operation wound was healed and I didn't have to wear the plaster anymore, I used to go fishing, swimming and to the gym with my foster father, that was during the summer holiday. Once school started, I went to high school, learned English and started to study Maths, Science, Biology, and Geography. I also learned more about girls, and I was getting more and more interested in them. That's when I really fell for a girl in my Science class, her name was Clarissa. She was the most beautiful girl of my age I had seen up to then. She had very beautiful olive skin colour, amazing brown eyes, beautiful brown hair and a voice that melted your heart – it certainly melted mine! There was one problem...my English was still not great, I could not hold a decent conversation, especially with the girl that I really fancied. In spite of that, we were still very close, we could hardly wait to see each other in the next class; it was a very nice chemistry between us, but I never asked her out. One day she came to me after the Science lesson was over, and she asked me: "Vas do you want to go out with me?" I didn't know what that statement meant, and I thought that she was inviting me outside in the school playground. I said "no because it's too cold outside". I could see she was a bit baffled, she kept quiet, turned around and she went to her friends. She was a little bit distant after that day. It wasn't until about 6 months later when I really learned what "do you want to go out with me" meant, that I realised what I had missed – I was gutted!!! It was too late to do anything by that time.

Life just moved on... From 1998 onwards I decided to concentrate on doing something more with my life, so I worked hard at school and college, as well as outside studies; I took up table-tennis, gym, swimming and fishing. In 1999 I entered a table-tennis competition, in London, for disable people, and finished second place.

At college I studied, GCSE English, GNVQ Business Studies and AVCE Information and Communication Technology. After College, in 2002, I went to University and studied HND Information Technology and Business & Marketing. I loved College, but University was even more amazing: the freedom to choose your subject and be responsible for your own results was very appealing to me.   Whilst I was studying, both at college and University, I was working part-time as well. I wanted to prove to myself that I was capable of being self-sufficient. I didn't want to rely too much on people helping me out...

Finding a Job

I remember applying for my first job when I was in college. Just like any other nineteen year old, I had these fantastic, unreal expectations and ideas about life and everything else. But a job hunt was going to change all of that.

I started listing the jobs that I was interested in and calling companies and agencies for an application form. Within a week or two, I started receiving calls inviting me for interviews. It seemed that I had all of the skills and qualifications needed for the jobs that I was interested in.

I was quite confident that I would get a job after a couple of interviews, and start working in a week or two given all the positive responses. My first interview was for the position of an assistant to a manager in a sales company. The interview was going well until I was asked, "Are you capable of getting up from your chair and collecting printouts from a printer?". I looked at him with an amused expression on my face. I did not answer because I was quite sure that he was joking. But he seemed to be waiting for an answer. "Yes, I can", I replied. Then he went on to say, "Give me a demonstration". I did give him a demonstration, but he said "someone will call you if you are successful", and the interview was over.

I got over the humiliation of this experience, and went for another interview the very next day. I was quite convinced that my first interview was just one bad experience, and I was not going to encounter such mindsets from other people. This was modern day Britain after all!

I went in for the second interview and this time, there was no interview at all. The interviewer was reading my CV when I entered his office and the moment he looked up, he just put the papers down and said, "Mr. Onica, I am afraid the position was filled internally". I consoled myself with the thought that it was just one more bad experience – of course people would not turn me away just because I was on crutches.

But they did. Every single time. I would get a call with an enthusiastic voice telling me that my qualifications seemed promising and that I should immediately come in for an interview. And mysteriously, by the time I came in personally, the position was no longer available.

It was utterly frustrating because I was not even being given the opportunity to be interviewed. I suspected that this happened just because I used crutches to walk. I went in seventeen times for different interviews only to be told that the position had already been filled. What I imagined would be a two-week process to find a job stretched out to a month and a half.

The recruitment agencies when challenged, would tell me that they had one spot left and I would have to appear for a preliminary interview. And the first question in the interview would always be about my disability. The interview would wind up in about ten minutes and none of the questions would be directed at my qualifications. Then I would be told, "We will call you and let you know if you have been selected for the final interview, and if you don't hear from us, then you did not make it". I did not get any phone calls later.

Finally, after two and a half months, I landed a job as a CD packer in a factory. It was the only job I could get. That was in July 1999.

I had just received a crash course in rejection.

We often make judgments about people's capabilities based on our perceptions about them. When we see a blind man, we often feel pity because we are certain that his life is full of struggles and he has no chance of achieving anything significant. Yes, his life is full of difficulties that we cannot imagine, and the things that are easy for us are amongst his biggest challenges....but a life without struggles is not always beautiful, and an easy life is not always beautiful either. If you are willing to take on the challenges then you are capable and, meeting those challenges takes on a special beauty of their own.

In my case, people are often quick to make judgments like this. They seem to think - "He is disabled, so he is not capable of anything". I have fought this bias all my life and will carry on fighting it to my last breath. We live in a society that apparently wants to help when we have to tick the box called 'disability' on application forms. But a tick in that box somehow tells the reader of the form that you are not capable, and cannot meet challenges. Isn't it sad that a tick box that is designed to be helpful can be read as a sign that you are helpless, and probably hopeless?

My crutches seemed to be the sum total of my abilities. It is extraordinarily difficult to change this mindset. I have discovered that the best way to deal with it, is not to. My abilities are only challenged by the reach of my dreams and my willingness to achieve them. It is sad that the people who interviewed me seemed to ignore my qualifications, and took it upon themselves to judge my abilities on the basis of the fact that I walked with crutches. Those people did, at least, teach me one thing – it was this: I must not weigh my worth against opinions of bystanders. It really is not worth it.

I have suffered personal losses, and experienced hurtful comments to the extent of being treated like an outsider on numerous instances just because I come packaged with a set of crutches: they are both a remainder and reminder of something that happened when I was an infant. Perhaps the advantage was that it all happened when I was very young. I was too innocent to grasp the difficulties that lay ahead of me. Why was that an advantage? Well it just did not occur to me to bear a grudge: as a young kid I just got on with life as it was, not as it was going to be. The weight of my crutches was the only additional weight I was willing to carry. Everything else seemed unnecessary.

But I was still keen on having a regular, perfect life just like everyone else. At that moment, I promised myself that I will find another way to have the life I deserve, with everything that is left in me - the moment I promised this to myself as I recovered from the surgery, my life changed.

You can struggle, you can dream and you can do everything that you are capable of, in the hope of achieving something. But sometimes, no matter what you do, it just won't be enough. What I learned was that sometimes, that is just how things will be. But it does not mean that you give up on everything. When you reach a dead-end, you need to change your path, and somehow, trace that new path to the end you want to reach. And if this one ends abruptly too, you find another. Don't ever give up, pursue your dreams. If the path you started on was not the right one, find another way to get there. When one dream dies, dream another dream, but never, never give up!

PART 3

CLIMBING MT. KILIMANJARO

04/03/2010 - Celebrating reaching the top of Mt. Kilimanjaro, with two of the amazing porters which looked after us extremely well.

Chapter 12

Another Dream Was Born

"All of our dreams can come true if we have the courage to pursue them." – **Walt Disney**

Trraanntiiing, trraanntiiing! My mobile phone's alarm went off. I woke up with a start, like I did every single day. It was 6:30 in the morning. Why was it already beginning to feel like the previous day?! How was I possibly going to get through another day that was in all possibility, going to turn out like all the other days that had gone by in that week? I had had a good-ish eight hours of sleep but suddenly, I felt exhausted at the thought of having to go through the same boring routine of my everyday life again.

I followed a similar routine every day. Most of the time I got very angry with myself for having such a boring life; I would wake up early, get washed and dressed, leave home for the office, start working, take a break, get back to work, have lunch, get back to work again, go to the gym sometimes, go home and wrap up everything before I hit the bed. I performed all these actions in the same order, and at the same time day after day. This had been going on for so long, that now I could even tell the time based on what activity I was performing! My life had become a habit. Stuck in a time worp, I was living the same day over and over again. It was as unremarkable as things could possibly be. Yet, it was comfortable. It was so comfortable that it got uncomfortable!

I logged on to my computer one evening after another mind-numbingly boring day at work. I was hoping to find something; a book, a DVD or a program that would bring some excitement and more fulfilment into my life. I came across the same annoying and cheesy websites, books and DVDs which offer the answers to all your problems: how to get rich overnight, fulfil all your dreams, and have everything you ever wanted – and be happy at the same time. Do you know the ones I mean? You have probably come across those before. All you have to do is buy them, wait for them to arrive, read them or watch them and then your life will be perfect! What annoyed me the most about these materials was that the authors were convinced that they knew better than I did what I needed in order to have a happy life. I can't blame them for making such bold statements, after all they have to make a living too – and have a happy, fulfilled life!

I switched off my computer in frustration, and had a few quiet minutes to myself. The unconvincing websites and materials which I had just read had put me off and, as I sat on my chair, I started thinking about how my day had been. There was an awkward silence in my head. I could not remember driving to work or what the outside weather conditions were. I could not remember a thing that I had done or seen! What the hell! Did I go to work today? Yes, but the only thing that I could remember was complaining to my work-mates how boring work and life were.

I had been doing the same things over and over again for so long that my mind seemed to be on autopilot: I was going through the motions of life, without it making any sort of impression on me: and I wasn't making any impression on the world, either! I was living my life as an obligation, nothing more.

But all this time, I had thought otherwise. I thought I had a near ideal life. The direction in which my life was headed was being solely steered by me. But suddenly, it dawned on me that the direction I was moving in, was just a flat line. I was barely doing anything at all. What was so worthwhile about my life? The fact that I had a steady job in a prestigious multinational company. The fact that I was going to the gym with my best friend, a few times per week – I was keeping fit, eating well, and investing all my savings on the stock market. I also had a beautiful girlfriend too! I thought that this was how a happy life was supposed to be, but I was confused as to why I did not feel satisfied.

Things were perfect and they had lulled me into a false sense of security. The fact that there were no problems in my life, was perhaps the biggest problem of them all. Life had lured me into its cosy arms and I was not even complaining because it was convenient that way. I did not have to face any new challenges or do something that would make me explore new things, *I did not have to do anything that would take me out of my comfort zone. I was doing the same things* over and over again. I did not have to think about them – I just did them mindlessly, and with little effort. I knew them well and there was no need for me to put in any extra effort to do them. I wanted the comfort that comes from being in a familiar situation. I was just being lazy.

But now I had woken up with a jolt. It was the moment of truth. I suddenly realized that I was living a life that left no traces – not even in my own mind. What if many years from now, as an old man, I turned around to look at the life I had lived, and remembered nothing? What if I had not done anything worth remembering? What if no-one remembered me...because they had not noticed me, and I had made no impact on their lives?

A-a-a-a-a-gh!! I had to change things and take control of my life. The way I lived my life would become my legacy, something that people would remember me for. And the fact that I lived an easy, comfortable life was not going to become my legacy.

I had to find a cure for the "disease" that I had allowed to take over my life; the "disease" of having accepted that life had nothing more to offer and I had nothing left to achieve. I needed to feel uncomfortable. And I urgently needed to feel unsure. I needed a challenge. I wanted a life that was something more.

A few days later as I sat in my bed, I started thinking again about my desire to change the course of my life. What could I do? What could possibly make me feel alive again? Several days had passed since that evening when those websites had got me thinking about my life. I had been wondering how I could fix my life ever since. I had been struggling to find a goal. Once I had a goal then I could find a way of achieving it. Right now I didn't have a goal – so it was not surprising that I had no sense of direction.

I kept thinking about a television programme that I had watched a few months back; February/March 2009. It was one of the most inspirational things I had ever seen..."5895 metres, five days up and two days down, and the ultimate test of human determination and grit...", I still remember the voiceover that played to the majestic views of Mt Kilimanjaro. A group of British celebrities had decided to climb the highest mountain in Africa to raise funds for a charity – the 'Red Nose Day'.

There were five episodes left when I discovered the programme, and I had watched each one. I used to rush home from work to catch every moment of their struggles as they braved extreme weathers and their own faltering will to conquer the peak. Set against the jaw-dropping views of the stunning mountain, I felt their pain. I shared their hardships, I felt like I was there with them. I knew their despair. Their struggles reminded me of times when I had fought my own battles...

It was absolutely awe-inspiring despite occasional helpings of cheesy melodrama. "It was way more difficult than I had imagined it to be", one of the celebrities had remarked. "It is the hardest thing I have ever done", said another. All of them seemed to complain about how hard it was. I had wondered, "This can't be so tough, surely; they are exaggerating! I could do it easily". That was one of those voices that you get in your head – something put these exact words into my mouth: "I could do it easily".

I felt I could do it easily because I had fought similar battles as a young boy back in Romania, way before I moved to England. I used to trek 4000 metres to my school every day. My house was on one side of the hill, and my school, on the other. I had to trek up and down the hill every day for an hour and a half just to reach my school.

I remember one particular day when the sun was absolutely ferocious, and I was trudging up that hill to attend school. Midway through the climb I thought that I would collapse in the heat. I had emptied my flask of the last drop of water it contained, and I still had more than half way to go. I felt like giving up on school, but I carried on and tried to forget about the heat of the sun!

As I made my way up the dry, barren surface of the hill, squinting because of the harsh rays of the sun, I stepped on a *piece of broken glass* that cut deep into my foot. The soles of my shoes had worn out completely and they did little to protect my feet. It would have been so easy to turn back and go home because I had cut myself badly, but I could not miss school that day as I had to be there because we had audition for the play that was part of the end of year celebration – it was more like a pre-selection for being selected for a play. My parents and teachers would have been really annoyed and disappointed with me if I missed it. I was going to make my mum and my tutor very proud. So I took my crutches, got up, and continued walking after wrapping a handkerchief around the wound.

I had walked my way up and down the hill so many times before, and in all kinds of weather too – blistering heat, freezing cold, and even torrential rains. And I did not even have the luxuries that the celebrities in the programme enjoyed. My parents could not afford them. My raincoat, sweater and shoes were just held together by a lot of patches. And I was barely seven at the time.

So with all this experience behind me, it is perhaps, not surprising that every time that I thought about the programme and Mt Kilimanjaro these past few days, I told myself that I could do it easily. And I genuinely believed that I could when I had watched the programme back in March – but somehow I had put it to the back of my mind and I had not given it any more thought.

But suddenly, as I thought about my life that day, telling myself that I could easily climb Mt. Kilimanjaro. I asked myself a question, "If you are so sure that you can easily climb it, then why don't you do it? You have done enough talking and thinking already. It is time that you walked the talk". I was stunned for a moment. The answer had been lying in front of me all this time. It seemed so easy and it felt so good! I made up my mind instantly.

This was the challenge that I had been looking for. Whatever else, climbing Mt Kilimanjaro would get me out of my comfort zone! Once I had decided that I was going to climb the mountain, the idea got hold of me. I was so excited. I thought about climbing Kilimanjaro. I dreamt of climbing Kilimanjaro. I talked about it to anyone that would listen. The mountain took over my life. I knew that I needed to do something with my life, to challenge myself and break old habits. The answer was at the back of my mind all the time – and it excited me beyond my wildest dreams. I was going to climb Mt Kilimanjaro! My dream was born out of a need to do something more with my life, to challenge myself and to break the pattern of familiarity. I had no idea then, that it would grow to be much more. I was absolutely thrilled to have finally found the answer to the problem that had been bothering me for so many days.

I remembered the rubbish that I had received in the mail "Do you want to be a millionaire? Here's how to give up your job, buy a new house, have a fantastic car, and spend your life in luxury." Of course, it was all rubbish. The excitement of the Kilimanjaro challenge put into perspective all the rubbish that I received by email. Of course it would be great to have plenty of money, a luxury house, a fantastic car and endless free time. But feeling fulfilled in life is more than that. I knew that I had found the answer that could give me a sense of fulfilment, and no-one could sell it to me. It was inside me all of the time. Somehow I knew that I had discovered that I can get anything that I want....but only if I want it badly enough, believe in it, and set out to find it. I would need strength, self-belief, determination and courage to find the life that I wanted, and deserved.

At that moment, I realized that I had indeed found the key within myself that would open the doors to new and exciting challenges. I could get anything I wanted, only if I wanted it badly enough, believed in it and set out to look for it tirelessly, and stoped only once I had found it. I just needed to commit myself to the life I deserved.

Suddenly my glance fell on the alarm clock and it was 7:15. I was going to be late for the office! As I got out of my bed in a hurry, my mind still caught in the possibilities of achieving my dream, I landed flat on the floor – I really woke up then!

Dazed by the adrenaline rush and excitement, I had forgotten something. I reached for the long wooden frames that were resting on the side of my bed - my crutches.

Chapter 13

Being Stubborn

"Being stubborn can be a positive thing, or it can be a negative thing. It all depends on how you decide to use it." - **Vasile Onica**

I was on my way to the gym from work. The thought of climbing Mt Kilimanjaro had occupied my mind the entire day. I could barely contain my excitement. I had faced a tough challenge in the office the entire day, trying to concentrate on my work. Mt Kilimanjaro was all that I could think about. The thought that had struck me in the morning was more than a whim. I had to make it happen. *And I knew that I COULD. As a result, I knew that I WOULD.* All that was left to decide was, how would I do it? I had not yet told anyone about my intentions and I could just feel the excitement and anticipation bubbling to the surface. I needed to talk to my great friend and gym instructor Watipa. As I drove, my thoughts suddenly drifted to an old memory.

My thoughts trailed off once I reached the gym. My mind switched gears, flooding my senses with visions of what lay at the top of Kilimanjaro. At that moment, I did not know how many days, weeks or months would pass before I could attempt to conquer that glorious peak, but I could still clearly see that goal in my mind - being at the top of Mt Kilimanjaro. I could see myself on the snow-capped peaks, happy, cheerful, ecstatic, feeling the warmth of the sun, smiling and content. I could even smell the air and feel the freezing snow. I had pictured everything in my head!

I have always been a dreamer. I don't just dream my dreams, I live them every moment of every day. I keep thinking about turning my dreams to reality. I keep working tirelessly to do everything possible to make them real. And if I feel like giving up on my dreams, I just imagine how it would feel to achieve my goal as my dream becomes a reality. And when I look at myself, happy and satisfied after my dreams have come true, it makes sense to keep working harder. And all the sacrifices that I have to make in order to reach that point seem worth it.

Some people have told me that my dreams are too unrealistic. People have made fun of me for dreaming too big. A lot of people seem to think that since I have a disability, I am not capable of achieving anything. So my dreams and goals seem unreasonable to them.

But do I let that affect me? No, absolutely not. I know what I am capable of. I don't let my disability overpower any aspect of my life. My disability never gets in the way of my dreams. NEVER....NEVER! I say to myself; "Vas, you don't use your legs to think with. You use your head, and as long as that is working, it does not matter what people say or think."

I can afford to dream big because I have the will and the desire to make that dream possible. So when someone tells me that I cannot achieve something, I tell myself that he/she is wrong to think that way. I know that if I let these negative thoughts affect me, I will never be able to achieve what I want to. You shouldn't let anyone talk you out of your dreams… absolutely no-one!

It helps to be stubborn. It helps to be absolutely determined about getting what you want. It helps to live and breathe your dream long enough to make it seem like reality. You need to turn your dream into a desire so powerful that you obsess over it every single moment of your day. And then you act out that desire until you have broken down every barrier that you thought existed. And then you shatter all the boundaries that others thought that you could not pass. Then, you watch as the dream comes true right in front of your eyes. And you watch yourself become a better, stronger person.

As I grew up, I realized that being stubborn can, sometimes, be a good thing. It is important that you never lose sight of your dreams no matter what anyone tells you. Don't ever believe anyone who tells you that you are dreaming an impossible dream. As long as YOU can dream it, YOU can achieve it!

Ok, I accept that sometimes I have not succeeded. Sometimes my dreams have not become realities but, every dream that I have dreamt, whether I have succeeded at it or failed, has defined me in some way. The experience has helped to reveal a part of me that I did not know was there!

There was no doubt in my mind that I would make this dream come true, that I would climb Mt Kilimanjaro. It was only a matter of how long before I did.

When I saw Watipa, my close friend and committed trainer, I told him about my dream of climbing Mt Kilimanjaro. I was not sure how he would react and despite my conviction that I was going to chase my dream at any cost, I needed him to say, "Yes! Let's do it!", but what if he did not believe that I could climb that mountain, and dismissed it as a childish and foolish thought?

With just one statement, Watipa drove all my doubts away. He said, "If there is one man capable of doing this, it is you". And that was it. That was the only thing I needed to hear from my close friend. With his support, I was all set to go ahead. I was not going to back down, not now. I was going to climb Mt Kilimanjaro, on crutches, no less. I still did not know how I would do it, or where I needed to start to translate my dream into reality, but with a clear sight of my goal, I was sure that I would find my way.

I was going to climb Kilimanjaro. I had no idea where to start, or what to do to make this dream a reality, I just wanted to do it at any cost. When the destination is clear, the why and the how of getting there are just minor questions. I knew the question: it was "Am I going to climb Mt Kilimanjaro?" I also knew the answer "Yes!" The alternative was not even on the cards. I would NOT take "No" for an answer: it was far too late for that. I had made up my mind and nothing was going to stop me! The journey had begun!

Sometimes, we let go of our ambitions and goals because we are not sure how we will achieve them. We give up even before we try to walk on the path that will lead us there because we feel that it is too tough, and we cannot possibly get through it. The path may be tough – after all it would not be much of a challenge if it was easy. The important thing is that we NEVER underestimate our ability to overcome the problems. But at the same time, do not ever underestimate your ability to overcome all the hardships that may come your way. The key to achieving all your dreams is a belief in yourself. And if you hold on to that belief tightly enough you will overcome everything that comes your way.

Here I was, aged 29, and behaving just like me aged ten: I was being very stubborn. I was going to make it to the top of Kilimanjaro. No question. No debate. It was going to happen! I had to make it to the peak.

I Had Made Up My Mind

The question, "How will I do it?", still remained. I had to figure out the path that would lead me to the peak. However, if you are a spiritual person, you will know that you should not worry too much about the 'how'...you will find that part once you know where you are going. That's what I did...I did not worry about the 'how'. Once I let that go, things started to 'just happen' for me.

I was at the railway station in London, waiting to meet my foster father, Dr Stuart Newton, who was coming back from his holiday. I think I surprised him a little bit with my opening line, "I have decided to climb Mt Kilimanjaro". I did not even ask him about his trip or a simple, "How are you?". I skipped the pleasantries and jumped straight to business. His pupils dilated and I could see that he was really surprised. I was almost expecting him to say, "What on earth is wrong with you Vas?", instead, he said, "That's great, tell me more".

My foster father has always believed in me and encouraged me to do what I felt I needed to, even if everyone else thought that I was crazy to think that I could. He has always told me that I should never let my disability limit the reach of my dreams, and I should always keep dreaming bigger and aim higher.

However, once I started talking about climbing Mt Kilimanjaro, he did not seem too supportive. It was as if he had forgotten his very words - "Vas, don't ever let anyone convince you that you cannot achieve your dreams". I knew that he was concerned about my safety and that was the primary reason he did not want me to go ahead. We had a heated debate over this for a week or two, in the course of which, everything that I heard, seemed to begin with the word "too"..."too dangerous", "too risky", "too cold". Nothing could change my decision though, for I had made up my mind to not just chase my dream but succeed.

Meanwhile, I had been thinking about ways in which I could make my dream more than just a personal journey. I wanted to reach out to people through my dream. I wanted to raise funds for a charity that worked for disabled people.

Moreover, I knew that if I could accomplish my dream of climbing Mt Kilimanjaro, I would be sending out a message to people that they don't need to lead the lives that society and conventional wisdom tell them to. I knew that reaching that peak would be the most powerful message that I could send out to others like me - "No matter what form of disability you suffer from, it does not have to take control of your life".

I found out about a British charity called Leonard Cheshire Disability, which helps disabled people worldwide. I decided that I would raise funds for them. They have a link with a travel company that enables people to take on unusual physical challenges around the world. This sounded very good to me. I looked them up and found "Mt Kilimanjaro challenge" on the list. I wasn't just happy, I was over the moon!

It seemed like things were falling into place on their own and gently pushing me ahead; it was almost as if my drive to see this thing through, was laying out the path for me. I still remember the exact layout of the website, it was one of the most happiest days of my life. Every step, no matter how trivial, was bringing me closer to my dream.

"I told you so!", I said to my foster father with a hint of victory in my tone, as I showed him the programme and the website. He finally gave in and conceded. It was at this point that he realized that I intended to move ahead towards my goal irrespective of what he thought. I was going to do it the way he had taught me, by ignoring everything and everybody who came in my way.

I could sense his discomfort and absolute terror thinking about all the ghastly things that could happen to me if something went wrong. I could see that he was only trying to protect me from possible dangers: not just being hurt physically, but also of being hurt emotionally too. I suppose he remembered some of the things that I had told him about my early experiences in Romania.

I could see that my foster father was trying to protect me from having to go through the pain of having to let go, all over again. He knew how hard it had been for me to get over the disappointment of not being able to become a footballer. What if I failed to climb Mt Kilimanjaro? All the anticipation and hope that had been building up within me, what if it was only preparing me for a bigger fall? He never voiced any of these thoughts to me, but I could clearly hear them. Despite our difference of opinions, he stood by me and it meant everything.

"How will I succeed if I keep thinking of failure?" - this has always been my philosophy in life. I knew that climbing the peak would come with severe consequences. I could get hurt. A lot of things could go wrong. But the fear of those consequences could not hold me back. The way I looked at it, there was no easy, painless way to do it. In order to realise my dream, I would have to make some sacrifices. And I gladly accepted that condition.

Moving Ahead With My Plans

It was time to move ahead with my plans to climb Mt Kilimanjaro. I contacted the charity and as expected, there were a lot of "ummms" and "ahhs". Although they did not say it, I could sense that the people who worked there thought that a guy who could only walk with the help of crutches could not possibly climb a mountain. But I refused to budge and kept pursuing them. After a few emails the travel partners, Discover Adventure, decided to give me a test challenge to see just how determined I was. The results of the test adventure would help determine whether

I was fit to climb Mt Kilimanjaro. They wanted to find out just how severe my disability was, and my capacity to tackle real physical strain. I would have to climb Snowdon to complete the challenge which, at 1085 metres, is the highest mountain in Wales.

You might think that, at this point, I would start training like a maniac to accomplish the task at hand. But I did not. I was extremely confident that my general fitness would carry me through. I went to the gym two or three times each week, so I was used to activities needing stamina and strength. I was also used to long walks to and from school when I was a kid in Romania: that had taught me about endurance when the surroundings were tough. I could already picture myself standing on the top of the mountain.

Days passed quicker than I expected. I was getting anxious and excited all at the same time. I was already thinking about climbing Mt Kilimanjaro because I was certain that I would make it to the top of Snowdon. I could not stop my thoughts leaping into the distant future. My excitement was hard to contain. It was only a few weeks since I had had the idea of climbing Mt Kilimanjaro. Just a short time ago the idea had seemed surreal, and now it seemed within my reach as I kept inching closer towards it.

The last few days before we began the ascent to the peak of Snowdon passed by me in a blur. I do not remember going to the office. I do not remember getting ready and driving my way to work. I do not remember anything except the picture in my head - on the summit of Snowdon.

I have had to let go of a lot of things in my life because of my disability ,and in every instance, letting go hurts. The more you have to let go, the more painful it gets. But, just because it is not easy to give up on a dream does not mean that you should stop dreaming. You need to dream and take chances. Most dreams are challenging – if they were easy they would not be dreams. The excitement of a dream is that it will push you to your limits. If you tell yourself that a dream is too difficult and that it will never become a reality you are short-changing yourself. The truth is that when you achieve your dreams, the excitement and sense of fulfilment that you feel makes all the hardships worthwhile. Even those hardships cancel out the misery you feel about missed opportunities if you have to look back at what might have been achieved if only you had made the effort.

Your dreams are kept alive by just one person - you. They are delicate and need to be protected, because they can be torn apart easily. So shield them, nurture them, wait till they grow their wings and then, let them fly. Making your dreams a reality will mean that you have to make sacrifices. If you are going to achieve a dream, then you will need to work at it, and that means less time for other things. When dreams seem to crash to the ground it is often because you are not willing to make the sacrifices. And you can't be sure that your dreams won't crash to the ground. But believe that they won't. And imagine that moment when they take on a life of their own. When your dreams soar, so will you. So do whatever it takes to breathe life into them.

The night before we were meant to leave for Snowdonia, I could not sleep at all. I kept thinking about climbing Snowdon, and no matter how many times I did, it never seemed enough. I lay in my bed for a long while, dreaming with eyes wide open.

Chapter 14

Climbing Mt. Snowdon

*"It is no sin to attempt and fail. The only sin is to not make the attempt." – **Suellen Fried***

We arrived in the beautiful country of Wales on 5th September 2009. We looked up at Snowdon - it was absolutely stunning. The entire landscape was bathed in a delightful shade of orange by the setting sun. A lush green enveloped the entire land. There was a distinct freshness in the air, a far cry from the fumes that I inhaled in the rush of the traffic back home, every day. I was really happy to be there.

We reached our hostel in the evening where I met the team who would be hiking along with me - the guides and my roommates. After dinner, we had a briefing from the guides about the two day hike. We were told what to expect and the mistakes that climbers often make. The guides also spoke about Mt Kilimanjaro and what to expect from the climb. After the briefing, I got to know the other members of the team before hitting bed early.

The next morning, I woke up to the pitter-patter of rain outside. The day of the climb had finally arrived. It had been raining and the landscape was tinged with a shade of grey, a tad gloomy, but beautiful nevertheless. We had our breakfast, and then set out to the base of the mountain in minibuses.

Once we reached the foot of Snowdon, my previously confident and sassy self took a back seat. I was feeling very nervous and I was beginning to think about too many things that ended with a question mark. "What if I don't make it?", "What if I fail?", "What if...?". The entire ride from the hostel to the mountain was plagued with concern and self-doubt.

By the time we reached the foot of the mountain, I could no longer think clearly. I made sure that I did not look at the peak because I did not want to intimidate myself. "Let us take this one step at a time", I told myself, taking a deep breath. The voices in my head were exaggerating my problems and making me nervous. I did not like the sound of it. I was losing focus. If I was going to climb this mountain, I would have to take control.

The team leaders quickly divided us into three groups of ten members each. Before we set off, the team leaders spoke to the members of their team again - we were told what to avoid. We were told the mistakes that all rookie climbers make. Obviously the leaders were trying to boost our confidence – and it worked! It was good to be able to laugh at some of the silly things that other people had done on the way up! Of course, I wouldn't do such silly things….would I?

Soon, we started the ascent.

Once we started climbing, I realized that I had grossly underestimated the effort required to do this task. My body had become accustomed to the comfort of an office life. The iron I pumped at the gym three times per week, was no match for the task at hand. I had been so confident about conquering this peak before I came here. And now, I was extremely doubtful about my chances of getting through this test challenge. Had I bitten off more than I could chew?

The rain had made the path very muddy and very slippery. It was an absolute nightmare because my crutches were getting stuck in the mud with every step that I took. Balancing on one leg, I had to pull the crutches out of a muddy hole every time I took one step forward. My arms were aching badly and I was falling well behind the rest of the group. And it was barely ten minutes into the climb.

I could hear myself breathing very loudly. I was really beginning to worry because we had only just started and I already felt exhausted. My mouth wide open, I was gasping for air with every step. I was struggling to haul my body weight with my crutches in the mud; my arms were going numb with the effort. My body was just refusing to go on.

"How could I possibly think that I was cut out for this?", I thought to myself. I looked at my watch and barely twenty minutes had passed since we started the trek. It felt like I had been climbing for ages. I wanted to stop; I wanted to forget about the entire thing and go home and sleep. But I did not. "You will have to make some sacrifices to achieve your dreams", I reminded myself. So I kept going, gritting my teeth through the agony.

One moment, I wanted to give up and several moments later, I would convince myself not to. I was breathing even more heavily; there was a riot of thoughts in my mind. "I cannot do this anymore"…"I must quit"…"What was I thinking?"…and then, another thought came into mind – the one that my parents had told me so often as they searched for someone to help me when I was a child.…"He can cure your son"…

I had to strive harder. I owed it to my parents for everything that they had done for me. They never gave up on me. So, how could I give up on myself? "Pain is temporary, but the guilt of giving up never is", I told myself. And even though this realization did not make the pain any less, it did give me a reason to bear the pain. And I started walking up Snowdon again.

My team was thoughtful enough to wait until I caught up with them. One of my team members, a girl called Marianna, gave me a warm smile and without uttering a word, or creating a fuss, took my bag away from me and carried it for the rest of the day. She was such a radiant and a positive person. We became friends as we hiked the mountain. Her words inspired me and helped me keep my spirits up despite my aching joints.

I had stopped looking at my watch. I was no longer in a rush to finish. I was not going to give up. I no longer cared how many more hours I would have to struggle; I was beginning to enjoy the journey. We were hiking to the sounds of gushing waters in streams all around us, and the raindrops hitting the tree tops and the surface of the earth. The more I let myself absorb and enjoy each moment of the climb, the more the struggle seemed worthwhile.

At the very beginning, I had promised myself to take this one step at a time and before I even realised it, I had taken enough steps to reach the half way mark.

We were supposed to cover half of the total height on the first day and then return to our hostel. It was meant to condition us for the climb to the summit on the second day. "How would I be able to do this all over again tomorrow?"...

A couple of hours and much soreness later, we started the descent. We had tested our stamina to the limits on the way up and, as a result, it was much harder and slower on the way down. The ground beneath me felt like quicksand, ready to gulp down my crutches at any moment. My arms were burning with the effort and I could barely feel my 'good leg', as I call it. But, my mind kept me going; "You can do it Vas", I kept chanting to myself. I kept saying it loudly in my head, loud enough to drown any questions or doubts that might have arisen.

A few hours later, we reached the foot of the mountain. Despite being terribly tired, I could barely feel any pain because I was too busy soaking in the moment of having achieved the first part of my challenge. I knew I was going to make it to the summit the next day. I had put all the questions and doubts in my mind to rest. I was at peace with myself.

Once we reached the hostel, I was overwhelmed by the affection and appreciation shown by the entire group. "Whenever I felt too exhausted during the climb, I just looked at you going, and that was all the inspiration I needed", one of my team members remarked. I felt really happy and humbled that I had managed to inspire and motivate people. They all believed in me. But most importantly, I believed in me.

The next day, we reached the base of the mountain quite early in the morning. I had been feeling extremely confident because I knew what to expect this time. Unfortunately, the weather had decided to give us an extra challenge that day. It was raining heavily, and the wind was particularly strong. The weather just kept getting worse as we gained altitude.

We kept going in the blinding rain. We could not hear anything because of the howling winds and the heavy rains. I was almost knocked over a couple of times because of the wind. My crutches were covered in layers of mud, making it harder to walk. But, I never stopped. All I could think of, was my destination, and it lay right at the top.

Four hours later, four agonizing, yet marvellous hours later, I took my final step towards the summit, and as I walked through the clouds that swam lazily past us, I finally reached a spot where my entire group was waiting for me. They were absolutely ecstatic as I joined them. The cheers and the applause that followed made me want to relive the past four hours all over again. A surge of relief and satisfaction passed through my body. It was like an electric shock – and I loved it! I just let the feeling flow around me and through me.

I was completely drenched, shivering, and sore by the time I reached the summit. This was certainly a great personal achievement, but the fact that a bunch of people I had met only a day before were cheering me on with so much enthusiasm, made me realize that this was a far greater achievement - to be able to move people just by following my dreams.

One of my group members came up to me and said, "You have changed the way I look at life and I can't thank you enough for that". I had once tied myself to the hope of finding my place in the bigger scheme of things. Maybe, this was it. Perhaps, I could continue to live a life that would inspire people to live better lives. Perhaps, I needed to see bigger dreams, and then achieve them all. Maybe this is how I could find my place in the greater scheme of things - by helping others see their own potential for greatness.

We spend our lives chasing what we think we ought to, for reasons that we believe hold the key to our happiness. And when we have reached the temporary highs of getting promotion, or a new car, we may realise that the high is not quite all that we thought it was going to be – so we start looking for something more, something that will last for the rest of our lives.

And so we spend our lives always looking for the piece that will complete the puzzle of life. But we never find it, because the piece was not missing in the first place. We achieve satisfaction and fulfilment when we realise that the 'missing piece' is within us. It was always there, waiting to be discovered. There IS also another puzzle that we have to complete in life. But it is not inside: it is outside. We need to understand that we fulfil ourselves only when we work and share with others. We complete ourselves by helping other people to complete themselves.

Our greatest achievement lies in being able to live a life that can inspire others around us. A legacy that lives on long after we are gone, a part of us that will be passed on. It was a moment of absolute clarity for me, to realize what had been missing in my life and suddenly, it all seemed to make sense. I had finally discovered my place to fit in.

Chapter 15

Rejection after Rejection

"Never give up on what you really want to do. The person with big dreams is more powerful than the one with all of the facts." –
Quote from Life's Little Instruction Book

On our way down, we took a break to admire the panoramic view, spread out in front of us. Our team leader pointed at a huge peak that stood out majestically and remarked, "Mt Kilimanjaro is seven times higher than that peak". One of my team members turned towards me and asked, "Vas, you think you would be able do that?". "Easily!", I replied with a cheeky grin.

 I woke up as my dream ended abruptly. It had been a week since I had returned from the training challenge and every night I seemed to dream about what had been and what was to come.

 And then came a major blow. After coming back from the Snowdon test, I waited for the travel company's report on me, about how I did and if I "qualified" for Mt Kilimanjaro. I was very excited to hear if I was good enough to travel to Tanzania. A day after I got back home, I received a phone call to say that I did really well on the

Sndowon challenge, but that I was a bit too slow. I think it was Dave at Discover Adventure I spoke to. He said that they needed to speak to their trip doctor and then have the doctor decide. So...I waited, and waited. After nearly two weeks of waiting, I decided that I had enough of waiting. By this time I could feel that there was something wrong here. So I emailed the charity and told them that the travel company seemed to have gone quiet on me, and that I have not heard from them for nearly two weeks. I also told Mandy, at the charity, that I felt these guys were trying to avoid taking me to Kilimanjaro. Eventually we: I and Dave talked, and I was told that the organisers were not sure that it was a good idea to have me with them. Despite the fact that I had successfully completed the Snowdon challenge, they were suggesting that I should call the whole thing off. I was devastated. Could this really be happening? Was it the end of my dream? No, no, no. I decided that I would climb Mt Kilimanjaro, and nothing was going to stand in my way. I emailed back the charity – Leonard Cheshire Disability, and told them about what the trip organisers had suggested. I can't remember what I wrote in that email, but someone from the charity called me back and asked me to get in touch with the organisers again. So I emailed the trip organisers and told them that I was asked by the charity to get in touch with them...

Now, it looked as though my dream of climbing Mt Kilimanjaro was about to be killed because some nameless person had decided that I could not do it. I was devastated that anyone could kill that dream. The great news is, that when I was feeling most desperate and most fed up, I received a response to my email from the travel company to tell me that someone had had a change of mind. In the space of a week everything fell into place and I climbed from the depths of depression to the peak of my dream – and I had not even arrived at Kilimanjaro yet!

I started training almost as soon as I got the news. I could not afford to take this lightly, not this time around. The Snowdon hike made me realize that I needed to work hard on improving my endurance and overall fitness. I started hitting the gym more regularly and doing intense workouts with my trainer Watipa who absolutely believed in me. He pushed me hard, almost always to the point where I started cursing him. His drive to see me succeed and achieve my goal was heartening.

Meanwhile, I also needed to figure out a way to raise money for my charity. Like everything else, I found my answer on the Internet. I found an online service where I created my account and added my affiliation to Leonard Cheshire Disability. I spoke about the challenge that I was going to undertake and requested people to donate if they identified with my cause and believed that I could complete the challenge. Any donations made to my account would go straight to the charity. I used social media to invite family, friends and co-workers to my page. Then, I waited for people to open their hearts...and wallets.

The next day when I arrived at the office, I expected the normal greetings but, instead, I got this – "How is the training going on Vas?", and then, "Do you think you would be able to do it on crutches?", and this, "Don't you think that you have set yourself too hard a challenge?", and finally, my personal favourite, "Don't topple over and break something, ok?". All these questions chased me for the whole day – during lunch, at the coffee machine and even in the toilets!

Everyone in the office had seen my charity page. And that day, I was the hot topic of conversation in the office. But I did not really like the attention. I could sense that a lot of my co-workers were particularly amused by the idea of a disabled person climbing a mountain. But I had no time to waste thinking about what they felt.

Meanwhile, the training sessions had started to grow on me. I loved every minute of getting out of breath and feeling as though my heart would just stop and I would drop dead any minute. I loved the fact that despite my body telling me that it was time to stop, Watipa, through his words, would motivate me enough to do two more repetitions of a set. Every time, I felt too tired or wanted to give up, Watipa would remind me why I was doing all of this, and that just kept me going.

I had been checking my donation page every day for weeks and the donation total kept growing because so many people were being kind and proving their belief that I could do what I had set out to. My family and friends were rooting for me, absolutely certain that I would make it, no questions asked. How many more reasons did I need to stay motivated? Absolutely none. Except, there was one more - kindness of strangers.

When a person who does not know you at all, reaches out to you in an act of faith, it is an extremely powerful thing; it makes you want to believe in unicorns and fairies, it makes you want to believe in everything that sounds ridiculous and unbelievable. A lot of people reached out to me over the Internet, people whom I had never seen or known, and I never would, but who still seemed to believe earnestly that I could climb Mt Kilimanjaro.

With a demonstration of faith in me such as this, I was moved and motivated.

But, every story has its villain. Wouldn't the world be a better place without their evil laughter and meanness? Maybe, maybe not. Everything has its place in the puzzle, villains included. The villains in my life have often threatened to outnumber the heroes. For every kind stranger who reached out to me, there were twice as many mean people who felt that I was a phoney who was 'playing the disability card'. Some also felt that I was a 'worthless piece of shit who should get back to his worthless life'. Bullies have always been drawn to my crutches. They will never leave my side no matter how old I get. Some of them said that I was raising money to pay for my trip, and that I was using a charity to cover up. But I always managed to cancel out their scepticism by providing proof that everything was legitimate, and that I did not need someone else's money to pay for my trip. Somehow there is a great satisfaction when you prove the sceptics wrong. Obviously our aim in life is not to prove anything to anyone, except ourselves. As long as you have a clean conscience, it does not matter what others think; most of them are just jealous because they cannot do what you can do, or are not willing to make the effort to try.

Know What You Want

Meanwhile, two months into the physical training, and the gym had become my second home. I had grown absolutely comfortable with the entire process. And that made Watipa extremely uncomfortable! He felt that if I got too comfortable doing something, it was time to take it a step further. So, one weekend, Watipa called me up and asked me to meet him at the hills near my home in Peacehaven near Brighton. If only it was a picnic that Watipa had in mind...I ended up trekking six miles up and down the hills.

I returned home that day absolutely exhausted to find two interesting e-mails; one from a British national newspaper and one from a Romanian tabloid wanting to interview me. I am not entirely sure how I felt at that point. One part of me was very pleased by the publicity, but another part of me was concerned that if someone wrote a story about me on the newspaper, I would have to succeed, otherwise they really would think that disabled people cannot do anything. I have always tried to succeed because I am not afraid of challenges, this time was no different. Actually, if I think about it, this interview gave me even more reasons to succeed!

Yet, I cannot run away from the fact that some of my failures let people question my ability to succeed. And that matters to me. But what matters more is the people in my life who will always believe in me, irrespective of my success or failure. Every time failure has looked down on me, I have brought myself up by thinking about all those people who care about me, the ones who have believed in me and the ones who will stand by me not because of my successes or failures but for my belief that I will never stop chasing the best that lies in me.

And yet, failure has never been an option for me. Failure would confirm people's beliefs about my abilities, or lack of them. There is only one way I can answer all the raised eyebrows and doubtful glances without speaking a word – by succeeding.

Every single time, with anything that I try to do, every goal I try to accomplish, I have everything at stake. I need to succeed every single time, time after time, because if I do not, I provide evidence to the doubters. Success is the only choice I have got. But my success speaks louder to me than it does to everyone else; it tells me that I am sane to believe in myself, it tells me that I have the power to live my dreams, it tells me that I can be everything that I want to be.

I could have dropped the idea of an interview with the reporter, but when I thought about it, I decided that it would let me reach out to a larger number of people and send them my message. Maybe, a little boy on crutches somewhere would get the assurance that things would turn out to be fine for him too, someday, somehow, even if everyone else laughed off his ambitions as a joke. But I would take that chance for that one boy, whoever he was. So it was in the end an easy decision for me. I immediately responded to the e-mail, "Yes, I will be glad to set up an interview...".

Days passed, and then weeks, and then months; I was finishing the six mile treks in half the time it took me a couple of months back. I was pumping more iron and I was getting out of breath less often. The amount in my online charity account had risen tremendously. Everything seemed to be moving in sync with what I wanted, effortlessly.

I received an e-mail from the travel company one day; it was a list of people who were going to climb Mt Kilimanjaro with me. The first name on the list was Marianna and then followed a long list of people I had met and made friends with, on my trek to Snowdon. I was absolutely thrilled that I would be among friends, as I took on my most difficult challenge.

As everything sorted itself out, I often thought about the days and weeks ahead, as I arrived at Kilimanjaro, climbed it and reached the peak. I felt that wave of sheer joy hit me with all its might. I used to visualize myself on the peak, and let a wave of happiness spread through me. I want to make it to the top. That belief filled me with such passion that it consumed my thoughts at all times.

Our beliefs are shaped by our experiences. They evolve out of a need to deal with, and accept, the most challenging circumstances. These beliefs emerge from the need to stay afloat when it looks like we can sink if we don't try hard enough. Our beliefs arise because of our fundamental instinct to survive.

One such seed was sown early on in my life – I have always had a firm belief that I ended up using crutches because of some profound reason that would reveal itself to me at some point in my life. I was looking for the silver lining in my cloud. I never gave up on myself. I did not really have a choice. Over a period of time, I realized that my life was following the path of my belief. As long as I stayed true to my beliefs, my life followed suit. And so, my belief strengthened and became a way of life for me.

I knew what I wanted with absolute certainty and all I had to do was to take one step towards it, it bridged the rest of the gap by walking towards me.

Chapter 16

No Turning Back: Leaving for Kilimanjaro

"If you see the President, tell him from me that whatever happens there will be no turning back." - **Ulysses S. Grant**

6:00 PM. I was waiting by the Ethiopian Airlines check-in desk at London Heathrow airport for members of my team to arrive. I was there three hours before departure time. I was feeling extremely nervous and trying hard to distract myself. My foster father had just seen me off and I realized that my dream was about to happen. How did seven months go by so fast? What had I told that other journalist from a Romanian newspaper who had interviewed me? "I shall bring photographs from the summit". Sigh!

As I sat there, twiddling my fingers and fidgeting around in anticipation of what was to follow, my gaze fell on the bulging bag that lay in front of me. Sleeping bag, mattress, head torch, thermal wear, first-aid kit, medicines, spare crutches, clothes, climbing boots, lots of snacks and my favorite brand of green tea – I could set up shop there if I wanted to! I was busy admiring my ability to fit in half of my kitchen in one bag, when someone tapped me on my shoulder. I looked up and Ritchie introduced himself to me. He was our trek leader.

We shook hands and chatted about nothing in particular. Ritchie had this amazing positive vibe that just radiated from him. I could instantly tell that he would make a great leader. I also met Patrycja, our trek doctor who was with him. They were both very warm and friendly people and we hit it off right from the start. The butterflies in my stomach were calming down because of the encouraging and optimistic words from both Ritchie and Patrycja. They both knew how to put people at ease.

Within minutes, Joanna, Joy and Nanas joined us, my pals from the time I climbed Snowdon. A huge wave of relief came over me when I saw them. We were all very happy to see each other. Soon, more faces joined us, many familiar, most, not so. I was busy chatting with Ritchie when an unknown individual came and introduced himself as a member of our team. Then, looking at me, he said with a tone full of sarcasm "Is he coming as well?" Ritchie beat me to answering this guy... "Yes, he is coming, and he is going to make it" Ritchie said with a slight irritation in his voice. I could tell he did not like the sarcastic comment from this guy any more than I did! I was so glad that he was going to lead our team.

I had heard and seen it all before – the derision, a sense of superiority, that taunting look...

My Greatest Challenge

My greatest challenge was not the one I was going to undertake. It was the one that I had to live with every day. In Romania, I was often looked upon as a waste of space, someone who could not do anything on his own, and had to be taken care of by others. Too many people in Romania thought that disabled people did not have the right to lead a normal life, have a family, a decent job and a respectable place in society.

When I was a kid, I remember one neighbour who kept her own kids away from me because according to her, "They will catch what he has got and end up crippled as well".

A lot of people felt sorry for me because of my disability. In fact, till the time I turned twelve, strangers in Romania would often come and offer me money because they assumed that I could not earn a living. I always had to struggle to be taken seriously. People often rush to my aid when I am trying to get on a bus or train, even though I am perfectly capable of doing those things on my own. Of course, I know that it is difficult for people who are not disabled. They do not know what to do for the best. Some gave me money with the best of intentions. Others helped me on to a bus or train, or gave me a seat so that I did not have to stand up: again they do it with the best of intentions.

What should they do? I confess, sometimes I don't know myself, but most of the time I wish they would just treat me as if I am capable, and not feel sorry or pity for me. Anyway, I am always very grateful for the fact that people show me kindness and consideration.

When I was eighteen, I remember that I was hanging out with my friends and we were heading for a bar. A girl came up to one of my friends and asked, "He is coming out with you too?!". She sounded rather shocked. My presence makes a lot of people uncomfortable. I do not fit in to the cosy little world that exists in their heads. The cosy little world where people with disabilities do not exist. How do I convince them that I have as much right to belong as anyone else? Perhaps the most important question that I should ask myself is, "should I even bother?"

All of these thoughts rushed through my head when I heard that team member of mine asking Ritchie the question he did, it reminded me of that girl, and so many other people who had previously asked me similar questions. I was not sure how to react or what to say.

Our entire team checked in two hours before departure time. With so much time to kill, we caught up with each other. It had been seven months since we climbed Snowdon. Everyone had their amazing stories and reasons behind wanting to climb Mt Kilimanjaro. Each one of us had dedicated the past few months in pursuit of that goal. We were an extremely optimistic bunch. We all shared the same vision and madness. We all wanted to reach the top of the highest free-standing mountain in the world, and do it for a good cause.

Two hours passed by in a blur of animated conversations. It was time to board the flight that would take us to Addis Ababa in Ethiopia, a seven hours journey. During the flight I was sitting next to Marianna, my friend from Snowdon, but I hardly remember talking to her. I am not even sure if I was awake the entire time. I was simply lost in my own world.

Pictures were shaping themselves in my head: Pictures of the summit, pictures of the glaciers beaming with delight in the sun, and pictures of all of us cheering and congratulating each other, ignoring the sub-zero temperatures. No matter how many times I thought about it, these pictures never got old or boring. They just kept growing bigger inside me, revealing more and more detail each time.

We finally reached Addis Ababa, in Kenya, and boarded our second plane to Kilimanjaro. Just over 2.5hrs later, we reached Kilimanjaro International

Airport. The moment we got off the plane, I soaked in the warmth of the place. The glorious African sun was an absolute delight. But I am not just talking about the temperature. There was a fantastic vibe about the place, maybe it was all in my head but it felt like home. It felt like this place was very familiar to me, like I had been living there.

We were going to stay the night at Moshi town, an hour's drive from the airport. We boarded the buses that were waiting for us outside the airport and took off. The views were absolutely exquisite. We could see Kibo, the youngest of Mt Kilimanjaro's three volcanic cones and the crater at the summit. Little farms and banana plantations covered the entire landscape. The people there seemed rather laidback and relaxed. "It is going to be alright", I could almost hear the words.

We arrived at our hotel, checked in, and almost immediately went out to buy souvenirs. A few hours later I returned with a lighter wallet and a lighter heart. It was already going well. We gathered for an early dinner after sorting out our kits for the next day - the first day of our climb. I was wearing a t-shirt that I had bought an hour earlier. It had a picture of Mt Kilimanjaro on it and the phrase - Just Done It! Almost everyone thought that I was being a bit cocky. It did not matter to me what they thought. I was simply reiterating my belief to myself, and the pictures I had in my head the whole time I was on the plane, training or at work. I saw and felt the end result.

After dinner we had a briefing from our leaders, and then we headed for our rooms. My roommate Jamie and I, checked our bags again to make sure that we had everything we needed for the climb. Jamie fell asleep soon afterwards but I still had a lot going on in my head.

I just could not get to sleep for a long time. I was restless and lots of questions passed through my mind; what if I could not keep up with the rest of the team? What if I had been too ambitious? I could not answer any of those questions without starting to climb Mt Kilimanjaro. I could not answer them if I stayed on the ground and limited myself to what other people expected of me. I had to set myself free, step out from behind those walls to seek the answers, and so I went to sleep knowing that I would be climbing the mountain, keeping up with the team, and getting to the peak putting all of those doubts to rest, once and for all.

Chapter 17

Day 1 – On the Mountain

The Fall left me Stunned

*"Our greatest glory is not in never falling, but in rising every time we fall." - **Confucius***

There are seven official treking routes on Mt Kilimanjaro. One of those is the Machame route and this was the one that we would take. This route is the most popular amongst climbers because of its wonderful views and the habitats of many sorts of animals and plants. The route has some very steep trails and is very demanding, so it is ideal for people who are physically very fit and have some hiking experience. Next morning, after breakfast, we headed towards the entry gate.

An hour's drive later, we found ourselves at the gate, completing the park formalities. We had to sign our names and passport details on a document which was kept by the Kilimanjaro National Park representatives. We were joined by our crew of porters at this point. While the park formalities were being completed, I stole a glimpse at the mountain. A lush rainforest spread out beyond the limits of my vision. I was trying hard not to get intimidated. I must have failed miserably, because Mark, one of the deputy leaders, came up to me and asked if I was feeling well. He assured me that I would make it. I gladly believed him and tore myself away from the majestic view to hear another briefing.

We started off very slowly even though the path was a gentle slope. We had been warned about being too enthusiastic because that way, we would get tired easily. We steadily walked through the lush rainforest on a winding trail. The path had not been taken by many people recently, and as a result, there was wild overgrowth all around us. The ground was slightly wet and muddy. A beautiful earthy smell rose from the place. The air was so pure that I just wanted to sit back and take in as much of it as I could. My senses were bombarded by the beauty of it all – the sights, the sounds, the smells – and even the tastes were overwhelming; it was thrilling and beautiful. I realised then how beautiful life and nature can be, and I ignored the worry or fear completely. It was sheer bliss.

After about two hours of hiking, the trail changed and the slope became rather less gentle. The gentle gradient had now given way to a steep incline. What had seemed like a walk in the park up until that point, was leaving us breathless now, as we had to walk our way up long, brutal inclines.

We stopped for a break after an hour during which, there was a slight drizzle, making the ground even more moist. I was glad to have the opportunity to rest. My shoulders and palms had started to hurt me because they were taking nearly all of my body weight. When people walk in the normal way they use their legs. The powerful bones and large muscles of the thighs and hips take all the of the body weight. My right leg could do some of that work for me, but my left leg was simply of no use – it scarcely reached the ground, so my crutches had to take most of my body weight, and my arms and shoulders had to take the strain. My palms were the connection between body and crutches and they were protesting!

We resumed after a while. I had barely taken a few steps when my right crutch slipped and the weight of the rucksack on my back pulled me back. I landed flat on my back with my legs going up in the air momentarily. My crutches took flight as well and crashed on the ground beside me. I did not get hurt and almost everyone, including myself, saw the funny side of it and laughed.

A few people came rushing in my direction, as always happens, to help me, but I propped myself up, using my arms, before they reached me. Like I always do.

We all start by crawling. Then, we learn to walk. I learned to walk when I was five. Till that time, I crawled up fences and trees, pulling my body weight with my arms: that helped me to develop plenty of upper-body strength, to make up for the weakness of my legs.

Crutches were an expensive accessory and my parents could not afford them. My uncle Costin made my first pair of crutches and taught me how to use them to walk when I was five. I was thrilled to bits. Until then I had had just one functional leg – and I could not walk with just one leg. Suddenly I had three legs to walk with!

The fall left me stunned, but also very grateful at the same time that nothing serious happened. Back in the UK I had often thought about the trek and the things that might go wrong. I had worried about incidents that could happen and put an end to my climb. One of those was the possibility of falling over and getting hurt. I had come so close to that on the first day! For the rest of the journey, I kept reminding myself to be extremely careful.

Each of us had two rucksacks, a heavy backpack carrying tents, mattresses and other heavy essentials, and a smaller rucksack with snacks, raincoats and, in my case, spare crutches. The heavier backpack was carried by a porter. I had to carry the smaller backpack. It was a cause of constant pain for me. It was an extra weight for me. Every time I tried placing my walking crutches forward, the rucksack just pulled me back. It made me very uncomfortable, especially, when I had to jump over streams or go over a rock that was higher than my knees. As a result, I was struggling to keep up with the rest of the team.

I guess Jo, the team leader, realized the difficulty I was facing because she assigned one of the porters to me, and he carried my small backpack too. I heaved a sigh of relief, as I could now just concentrate on the terrain without the worry of coping with a rucksack. I could sense that this did not go down too well with a certain part of our group. A lot of people, especially those who had not been with me for the Snowdon trek thought I did not belong there, and felt no hesitation in voicing their thoughts. I patiently waited for their opinion to change. I knew that it would in due course.

Before we could continue, I examined my crutches to check if any new scratches or cracks had appeared on them after my fall. And they had indeed. In fact, they bore the wounds of many such adventures.

I have a love-hate relationship with my crutches.

They are the reason that complete strangers make judgments about me before I even open my mouth. My crutches are one of the things that I have to battle against. Can you imagine how it feels when a friend tells me that a girl that I fancied said "If he wasn't on crutches I would like to go out with him"? Perhaps she thought that I was less of a man because I could not walk using both of my legs. Some people make comments like these without thinking. Some people make them deliberately to hurt. But comments like these caused me a lot of heartache as a child.

But, that is exactly the reason why I fight. My crutches remind me that I need to. They remind me that I need to try harder. They motivate me to stop at nothing short of having the life I deserve. They are the reason for the fire that burns inside me. My crutches remind me that I cannot take my life for granted; in overcoming the stigma that surrounds my disability. My crutches stand for possibilities. They are my reasons for being strong. They are the symbols of my spirit and determination.

Everyone needs something that will release his true self, and allow him to achieve his potential. Most of us struggle to find it. Some of us even lose sight of our potential as we tackle the everyday challenges of life. We have to accept what we are given and make the best of it. My crutches present their own challenges – but every day they are an obvious reminder to me of the importance of getting on with life and enjoying not only the challenges, but also the opportunities.

I smiled as I wiped my crutches clean of the mud and continued walking.

I had expected the first day of the climb to be easy and the slope to increase rather more gently. But I was wrong. It didn't. It was definitely far more challenging than I had imagined and I wondered what other surprises were in store for me over the next few days.

As the hours went by, the forest was bathed in stunning shades of yellow by the sun. Four hours later, we reached the Machame camp after trekking for 18000 metres. We were now at an altitude of 3100 metres above sea level. As the sun set, the temperature started falling rapidly. I was exhausted beyond measure and just gobbled up the food that was prepared by our porters. I could not wait to hit my bed. Yes, tomorrow it would be great to continue the journey but, right now, all that I wanted was a wonderful long sleep. I do not remember having much of a conversation with my tent buddy Jamie as I instantly fell asleep.

Chapter 18

Day 2

My Disability Is Not an Excuse

*"Ninety-nine percent of the failures come from people who have the habit of making excuses." - **George Washington Carver***

The next day, we headed to Shira camp from Machame, at an altitude of 3840 metres. Fortunately it wasn't a vertical climb – just a long steady path 9000 metres long, and it took us between four and six hours to complete.

Our route took us through the rainforest until, we reached the steep ascent onto Shira plateau. The forest was magical. As we walked past thousands of densely-packed trees they seemed full of all sorts of noises from the animals that lived there: we didn't see them, but we heard them chattering and rustling the leaves. When we came to an open area we could look back and see the parts of the forest that we had just passed through: we saw the tree-tops glistening in the sun and nodding their branches gently in the breeze. In the distance we could see Arusha, a large town in the foothills far below, and rising majestically above Mt Meru and Mt Kilimanjaro. The rocks and peaks stood out boldly under the clear blue sky. It was a gorgeous sight and we all just stopped in our tracks to admire it.

While trekking, we talked constantly amongst ourselves - about our jobs and our lives...but a silence gradually fell over all of us when we reached that open area. We were lost in awe: the mountains were vast and beautiful, and we were so small. It was an unforgettable experience and helped to put the troubles and difficulties of life into perspective. Everything else seemed so ordinary.

We resumed our trek after what sounded like a thousand gasps and sighs, and the thousands camera clicks. I was annoyed at trailing behind everyone and pushed myself a little harder than necessary. I swiftly moved past everyone and would have continued had I not been patted on my shoulder from behind.

I turned around to find the guy who had ridiculed me at the airport. He asked me to stop so that he could have a word with me. I had no idea what was cooking in his mind and I hoped that it was not something unpleasant. His body language suggested otherwise. I knew how he felt about me and I had decided to leave him to it. And I had hoped that he would reciprocate.

The man who had made some negative comments about me asked me to slow down. He said: "I hope you remember Ritchie telling us that Mt Kilimanjaro is notorious for causing altitude sickness and other assorted discomforts like headaches, and shortage of breath. This is because there is less oxygen and the temperature is lower than there is at ground level. The body takes time to get accustomed to these sudden changes in environment. Moving slowly is the best we can do to minimize the effects", he said. I remembered one of the briefings. He was right. I was making it harder on myself to acclimatize.

A few moments before I had been expecting unpleasantries from this guy – and here he was giving me kind thoughtful advice. The experience reminded me that is so easy to misjudge people.

A few more hours later, the pain that had been building up in my palms and shoulders since the day before, became acute. I was alarmed. Although the pain had been anticipated, this was just day two! I simply could not afford this. Crutches are not really designed for comfort. Years of use have taught me that there really is no pain-free method of using them. Even when walking on flat ground, my palms became rough and hardened, just like the soles and balls of the feet of other people. Now I had taken on the task of climbing a mountain, and the pressure on my palms was much greater. Although the skin of my palms was thick, the pain was significant. I had experienced this when I climbed Snowdon. The problem was that Kilimanjaro was steeper and harsher: climbing this mountain was much tougher on my hands and arms. My powers of endurance were being tested far more in climbing Kilimanjaro than in anything that I had ever done before.

While I was training to climb Mt. Kilimanjaro, I came across an African proverb that seemed to be designed for me, "Disability is not an inability!". I may be physically disabled, but I am not mentally disabled. I lack the use of one leg – that's the physical part. The essential thing that I need to remember when the going is gentle, or tough, is that a physical disability can be conquered if you are determined NOT to let it ruin your life. My disability is not about what I lack - the use of a leg. My disability lies in how much I let it affect the course of my life. I have discovered that when my body starts acknowledging its limits, my mind starts exploring and pushing the limits further.

I have never considered myself to be disabled, this is simply because I can do everything that I want to. My crutches have never become an obstacle for me. My family had an immense role to play in inculcating this value in me. My parents were left shattered because of what had happened to me, but they never let that overshadow my upbringing. I realize now how deeply it must have affected them, but they never let it show. They were going on with life as if nothing had happened; at least that's what they let me see.

As a child, I was treated just like my brother and sisters. I helped my mum with daily chores and my dad with everyday tasks like getting hay for the animals, feeding them or taking them out to the fields. I never felt disabled because my family never treated me as if I were disabled.

My disability is not an excuse, I reminded myself, and kept going.

We had now moved to open spaces with types of trees that I had never seen before, and the ground was covered with beautiful wild flowers. A cool breeze and a bright sun made for near ideal conditions for climbing.

We soon reached a part of the mountain that required us using our hands a little bit more to overcome it, after which, the path continued upwards, and a few hours later, we reached our second base camp, resting on a rocky plateau. By the time that we arrived there, it was noticeably colder – the result of the sun setting, as well as the higher altitude – 3840 metres.

It had been an amazing day, and as I sat reliving it over a cup of hot tea, I was approached by a member of our team that I had not spoken to before. He said: "The first day at the airport, I wondered how you would be able to keep pace with the rest of us. The first day of the climb, when we reached camp, I asked myself how much further you could go. Today, I know for certain that you will go all the way", he said earnestly. I did not expect such positive feedback so soon, but I was very grateful for it.

Chapter 19

Day 3

The Altitude Sickness Strikes

*"All the adversity I've had in my life, all my troubles and obstacles, have strengthened me... You may not realize it when it happens, but a kick in the teeth may be the best thing in the world for you." - **Walt Disney***

I woke up on the third day of the challenge with a massive headache and dizziness. It had started building up the night before but I had dismissed it, thinking that it would be gone when I woke up.

I had woken up during the night. It was about two in the morning and I felt a sharp pain in the nape of my neck: it was spreading upwards to my head. The pain woke me up, but I was too sleepy to register anything sensibly. I thought that I was dreaming about getting a headache!

It was clear now that I had not been dreaming the previous night. Everything around me started spinning at a sickening speed. I felt like I was going to vomit my guts out. As I reached for my crutches to hoist myself up, I lost balance and put out my right arm to break my fall: a jolt of pain ran through my arm! In just a few seconds all sorts of scenes passed through my mind. Was this the end of my hope to climb Kilimanjaro? Would everyone back home look at each other and say "I knew he couldn't do it"? I regained my balance and made a second attempt to get up only to find that I could barely stand. But I could not stay back and wait for things to stop spinning! We would soon have to start and I did not want to complain. I had already given people enough reasons to confirm their belief that I was a boy trying to do a man's job. I had no intention of giving them another.

I got out of the tent to join others for breakfast. Those few steps, felt more painful than the two previous days of trekking combined. With every step that I took, a blinding pain shot through my head, leaving me momentarily stunned.

I could no longer be my happy, enthusiastic self, despite my best efforts. Ritchie perhaps noticed this because he pulled me aside to have a word. He enquired if I was feeling alright and if I needed anything. "I am absolutely fine, just a little tired", I replied. He did not look too convinced though, but he left me to it.

I did not want to acknowledge any problem because I felt that the moment I did, it would take control of me. If I decided to let it grow on me, it would dictate my thoughts and actions, reminding me at each step that I could not go on because it needed my immediate attention and for that to happen, everything would have to be put aside. So I kept going.

After breakfast, we started walking towards Barranco hut, a 15000 metres trek. The character of the trek had entirely changed. Instead of rainforest, we were now on high moorland. This is an entirely different landscape. No longer were we surrounded by dense and colourful plant life: now we were trekking across large areas of rough and rocky terrain, between parched and arid desert areas. We had left behind the abundant colourful bushes and varied plant life that surrounded us on the second day.

That day, the weather was very changeable. One moment the sky was bright blue, and just a few minutes later it was dark grey. There was a strong wind that blasted us every step of the way – it screamed and howled at us like some demented ghost. It made walking extremely difficult and there were times when I felt that I would be thrown backwards. Our target, the peak of Mt Kilimanjaro, loomed over us, off and on, throughout the day. When we saw it, it seemed to be tempting us to go further, and then it disappeared from sight as clouds and mist surrounded us, or the top, or the region in between.

We braved the weather while moving across the southwest side of Kilimanjaro, passing underneath Lava tower at midday, a 100 metres formation that sticks out of the mountain. Then, we started descending the hill to make our way towards our camp at Barranco hut. This was very tricky as we had to scramble over rocks, most of which were loose.

It was getting hard for me to focus; my headache had been getting even worse as the day progressed. I had started walking with my head buried in my chest in an attempt to protect my face from the sudden gusts of strong wind and heavy rainfall. I was overcome by nausea as the ground beneath me swirled rapidly. I could not figure where or how to take the next step. I stood in one spot for what seemed like an eternity, unable to move or see. The only thing that my senses could register was the rain hitting against me, making the thumping in my head even worse than it already was.

I gathered myself and opened my eyes only to realize that I had been left behind. I had to catch up; I could not just wait there for the weather to get better, or my head, for that matter. Each step I took demanded all of the willpower that I could gather. "You did not come this far to give up", said the voice in my head, above the throbbing. But the voice kept getting dimmer.

There was just too much noise; my heart was pounding remarkably. The rain had unleashed itself mercilessly, threatening to shatter everything in its path. How much longer? I just kept going somehow. I could not reason anymore or question. I had lost my ability to. So I kept walking. Then after what seemed like ages, it stopped raining and the winds calmed down. A slight snowfall followed, and soon, the sun was out again. A few more steps later, I saw my team waiting for me at a distance.

As I bridged the gap, I realized that the headache was getting much worse – even though, in the morning, I thought that it was as bad as it could ever be. I was feeling sick and very dizzy but I did not want to shout out, not yet. As I placed my crutches in front of me to take a step forward, everything went out of focus. My crutches slipped, and I fell to the ground. My eyes tightly shut, I could hear people running towards me, and their voices were getting louder as they got nearer. My head still hurting, I propped myself up against a rock. The layers of clothing on me, had shielded me from physical harm. The wounds that I was trying to hide were of a different form anyway - part pride, part ego, part everything.

"I am absolutely fine. It was the terrain, I got a little distracted and put my crutches on a loose rock", I told everyone.

We continued soon afterwards, and barely a few minutes after resuming our trek, I fell a second time. It just seemed like all my senses were shutting down. It felt like I was standing in a closed space and the walls were collapsing around me. I did not know how much longer I could pull this off. I blamed the terrain again and continued. How much longer could I go? Maybe a little more.

We reached camp at Barranco Hut in an hour, at an altitude of 3983 metres. We arrived at a tin shack where we pitched our tents. The problems that I had experienced today were all about acclimatization. As we approached the summit the air pressure became lower and the amount of oxygen was less. That takes some getting used to! In one day our path had taken us up 690 metres, and then down 580 metres. Although I did not realize it at the time, we were taking one of the mountaineers' laws very seriously – 'climb high, sleep low'. That law helped each of us to acclimatize. However, I still felt the altitude sickness quite badly. As far back as I can remember, I have never felt so sick before.

Our porters had prepared lunch for us but I only managed to force a few morsels down my throat. How much longer could I go? No more. I could no longer pretend that everything was alright. I just could not take it any more. I decided to confide in Ritchie and Jo, our leaders. I was feeling so sick and exhausted that I went up to them, hoping to hear them say, "That's it Vas, you are too sick to continue on this journey". I had absolutely given up at this point and honestly, I no longer cared about anything. I was certain that I could not go on, and even more so, that I did not want to. But something did not feel right. The idea of me giving up at this stage did not feel right at all.

Our entire group was divided into two teams - one, headed by Ritchie and the other, by Jo. I was in Ritchie's team, and after lunch, our group was supposed to leave first. But after my confession about the discomfort I was experiencing, I was left behind with Jo's team: we were going to continue later. Ritchie left with his team after assuring me that it was going to be fine.

Jo convinced me to continue and not to give up. And despite my aversion to pills of any kind, I popped one for altitude sickness that she absolutely insisted on. I ate a little more with her encouragement and then started on that path once more. I was still not sure how far I could go but she seemed to have no doubt that I would go right till the end. Her belief kept me going. Jo and my close friends, Joy, Evelyne and Nanas were by my side the entire time, encouraging and supporting me. It made me want to carry on. It also made me realise how important it is to concentrate our energies, love and attention on people that are there for us no matter what. People that love, respect and encourage us in difficult times as well as good times.

The scenery that surrounded us was enchanting and it helped to calm my uneasiness. The alpine desert had fallen far behind and we had returned to the kaleidoscopic moorlands with their spectacular array of colours. Beautiful waterfalls cascaded down the valley as we descended our way to the camp at Karanga hut.

The weather continued to spring surprises on us: one moment it was pouring with rain, and another moment the sun was sparkling in a clear blue sky. Views of Mount Meru, the Heim Glacier and Kibo's south face were at the mercy of the mist that hung low for most of the day. But there were moments when every element played its part perfectly; the rains stopped and the mist cleared, followed by a shimmering sun and in that moment all the hidden views came out in full glory. It was breathtaking!

I was still struggling to tame the unrest inside me. Every step came with a painful baggage. My head was hurting so badly that I could barely keep track of where I was going. But my friends were there with me throughout my ordeal - Joanna, Joy, Nanas,

Jo, Ritchie, Mark, Jamie, Patricja and all the porters who I had made friends with. Their support did not make the discomfort magically go away. It just gave me a reason to bear it the best way I could because I did not want to fail them.

Of course, not everyone was on my side or as patient or kind. The mean guy from the airport was walking close to me and talking rather loudly. "That guy with the crutches is not going to make it and I am sure that he will pull out any minute. He seems to be rather unwell and on top of that, I doubt how far he can go with those", he said pointing at my crutches. I knew he wanted to make sure that I heard him. I did not know what his problem was, and frankly, I did not want to find out either.

I know that I will always be questioned because of my disability. It is looked upon as a weakness, a vulnerability. I do not satisfy the rules that society outlines for a regular life. I know that I will always be looked upon as the odd one out. I do agree. I stand out. But not due to my crutches. I stand out in spite of the fact that I am on crutches.

I could have answered him back. But I had seen too many of his kind before. So I knew it was not worth my time. And there was far too much optimism   surrounding me and urging me onwards. There were so many people around me who deserved my attention and respect, and I decided to give them every bit of it instead of dealing with just one person who was the exact opposite, and who seemed determined to pull me down with his negativity – I simply was not going to give him the satisfaction of finding out that he was getting through to me.

My headache had started getting better in the meantime. At the time I was not sure whether it was the pill or my friends' support, care and consideration. Thinking back to the events I am sure that it was a great deal to do with those friends. They pulled me through. They kept my spirits up and helped me find my self-belief again. An hour later, the sickness had entirely gone. I am deadly serious!

I found my enthusiasm again, certain that if I could overcome anything that Kilimanjaro could throw at me, I would go all the way. I can tolerate most degrees of physical pain since they are a part of my territory. I have been conditioned to accept them as a part of my existence. My crutches have meant that, over the years, I have had to deal with palms that were raw and sore. Even walking at a leisurely pace can be very uncomfortable after a time because my palms and shoulder muscles are taking strains that they were not designed for. Although I knew that climbing a mountain on crutches would not be easy, I had not realized just how nasty the pain and the strain would be.

We all have a comfort zone, and we do not usually want to leave it. If we want to try something new it means that we have to go to the boundaries of that zone, and enter the uncomfortable world of the unusual, unfamiliar and unknown. The trouble with challenges is that they are all outside of our comfort zones. When we are presented with new challenges, we often say "I can't do it", because we know it will be outside of the security of our comfort zone. "I can't do it" usually means "I won't do it" or "I'm not even going to try". We do so because we inherently dislike challenges. So we fiercely guard the boundaries that we ourselves create. But stepping outside those boundaries is often not as difficult as we thought that it would be. The moment those crutches became a part of my existence, I was forced to step outside my territory and step into another. The transition is the hardest part, I discovered. Once you cross over, it is worth the pain. You are no longer a prisoner inside the boundaries in your mind.

This happens so often in our lives. The first task is to recognize that the only answer to "I can't do it" is "Oh yes I can!". That's easy to say. So, how do we do it? Firstly we have to identify what the challenge involves – is it a challenge or a new opportunity? Either way there will be things that we have not done before – and the unknown always makes us uncertain. But take on the unknown. In reality it gives us the chance of infinite possibilities to grow and discover ourselves. The secret is to knock down the barbed-wire fence that we have built round our comfort zone – the fence keeps the comfort in and the unknown out. If we want to take our lives forward we need to let the comfort out and the unknown in.

The altitude sickness made me step out of that zone where everything worked in my favour. It was a wake-up call to remind me that challenges are not about everything going my way. I needed to find a way to take the challenges head-on and go past them.

Meanwhile, a few other members of my team had been getting worse as the hours went by. They were also suffering from altitude sickness, and had been throwing up badly; dizzy and barely left with any strength to walk on their own. They were struggling with the challenge.

By the time I recovered, three members of our team had decided to abandon the trip for good. It had a strange effect on my feelings. One part of me felt so sad for them because they had come all this way and had had to back out of the challenge. Yet another part of me was pleased that I had suffered and had come through the sickness. It was unfortunate that we had to leave our colleagues and friends behind. We said our goodbyes and continued.

As we passed through the valley that led to Karanga hut, where we were camping, the vegetation returned, and we passed through the 'Garden of the Senecios' which are characterized by extremely odd-looking plants. With Kibo looming large in the background and a massive rock face standing like a wall on one side, we trekked our way to the camp.

By the time that we reached the camp, our porters had already pitched the tents. After a cup of hot tea and equally hot dinner, I went to bed. It was really cold that night, a lot more than the previous two nights that we had spent on the mountain. My weaker leg was beginning to get really cold. I took out an extra pair of thermal socks and trousers from my bag. After putting on three layers of clothing, I cocooned myself in my sleeping bag. Although tired, I was struggling to fall asleep. I started thinking about my childhood.

Chapter 20

Day 4

Do Whatever It Takes to Overcome the Obstacles

"The greater the obstacle, the more glory in overcoming it." -
Molière

The next morning brought two unwelcome surprises for me. One was a severely infected toe on my right foot, and the other was a swollen and infected finger on my right hand. They were both unwelcome and worrying. My right foot was my good foot and took my weight. The infection on my hand was especially worrying because both hands were involved in supporting my weight through my crutches. There was I thinking that I had come through the worst of my problems of altitude sickness, only to be hit by infection! Fortunately the doctor was around and provided antiseptics. She was able to lance the infected areas and, with the help of some bandage I was able to put on my boots and gloves and take on the world!

We were heading towards the Barafu camp, an 18000 metres walking distance stretch that would require us to trek for close to eight hours by descending into the Great Barranco, a huge ravine, and then exit steeply up the Great Barranco wall that divided us from the south-western slopes of Kibo.

"The Barranco wall is a 300+ metres rock face. It will be one of the most challenging treks you will face on Mt Kilimanjaro and if you can get past it, you will easily get past the rest", I remembered one of the Snowdon trainers telling me. As we walked towards it, I was considering ways to climb it. It did not appear to be a tough or a technical climb but it would take a very long time. Even from this distance it was clear that I would not be able to use my crutches. How could I tackle the climb? My mind was in overdrive? If I climbed on my hands and knees, what would happen to my crutches? Ah, thank goodness for the porters. They would be able to take my crutches and then I would be able to ascend – slowly and carefully – but I would do it!

The ground was covered with loose stones on our way to the Barranco wall. Despite being extremely cautious, I fell face first as my crutches failed to grip properly, landing on my right knee. A bolt of pain shot through my right knee – my good knee – the one that took all of my weight. It was painful enough when I was down but, when I stood up and put my weight on to it the pain brought tears to my eyes, but I had to go on so I brushed myself off and continued walking pretending that I was not hurt at all. But I was. The muscles of my thigh and knee were trembling violently and I was just hoping that the pain would get better soon and that it was nothing serious.

I got up and continued walking but I fell again a couple more times, unfortunately hurting my right knee again, and again. The pain kept getting worse and I had to put on a knee strap before I could continue.

I carried on while chatting with my team members. No matter how much I tried distracting myself, the pain would crawl its way back to become the centre of my attention. My knee was hurting really badly but I did not see the point of letting everyone else know about it.

I did not want to explore the possibilities that lay on the other side of being badly hurt. I could not let anything come in my way. Perhaps it was a foolish thing to do...but the world would not wait for me to catch up. Or so I had learnt as a child. And I had certainly not come all this way to give up. So, I convinced myself that my knee was perfectly fine and that it would get better eventually. Except that the 'eventually' never really came that day. The pain just kept getting worse.

We had almost reached the Barranco wall and I still was not sure how I was going to do it. I had some ideas but I was not certain. It was a gigantic rock casting a shadow that covered the entire valley. The climb would have taken me three or four hours, even if I had not hurt my knee. But I had hurt it badly. I was not sure whether I would be able to cope with that climb and, if I did it would make my knee worse than it was.

As a kid, I was always getting cuts and bruises on my knees, and everywhere else. Of course, that's true for all kids. We fall over when playing football, climbing trees and doing all of the other things that youngsters do. Our knees, legs, hands and arms all bear signs of our little adventures.

I used to tie handkerchiefs around my knees and palms and stuff them with bits and pieces of cloth that I could find around my house, in the hope of making things easier and a little less painful. Yet, every day, I used to return home and spend time examining bruises, cleaning cuts and pulling out grit gained during my explorations. It used to hurt at times but those minor problems did not stop me from exploring the world again the following day. For all children, the sheer joy of being alive and investigating their world far outweighed the pain of a few cuts and grazes. Like all other children, I found that tomorrow would bring lots of new challenges – and so I kept on crawling on my hands and knees before I had crutches.

I needed all of that determination right now. We were at the foot of the Barranco wall and I still did not have any clear idea about how I was going to climb it. I just knew that I had to go over it somehow. I hoped that the path would show itself to me. I simply believed that it would.

The temperature was very low. This was largely because of the enormous shadow cast by the Barranco wall. Icy winds had been blasting us all morning and now they were hitting hard against my face. A hush had fallen over the entire group. I was eyeing up the rough line that marked the trail up the wall. I could not even see the end of it, it just disappeared high up in the clouds.

The silence was broken by one of the porters shouting "pole! pole! (slowly! slowly!)". We began hiking along the rocky trail, gaining altitude with every single step. The track would at times end abruptly, requiring us to do some rock climbing. I managed by giving up my crutches to whoever had climbed before me and then scrambling my way up. The first few times, I barely felt anything but soon my knee started acting up again as it brushed against the rocks while climbing.

As we climbed higher, the temperature was falling. It felt as though it was, at most minus 15 degrees Celsius, although the wind was probably helping to make the air feel more cold than it really was. But, even without the wind chill the temperature was certainly well below freezing. At one point, I turned around to find an absolutely stunning view of the Barranco camp partly clothed in the shadow of the wall. We had hiked a great deal in a short period of time and it had not been as bad as I had imagined. We kept going until we came across an almost vertical stretch of rock that we had to climb.

The local guides and the team leaders had already set up ropes that ran along the stretch by the time the rest of us reached there. Almost everyone in my team managed to get through this part smoothly with the help of a few leaders positioned at the top of the climb, pulling people up. Soon, it was my turn to climb. I wrapped my hands and arms around the rope and tried pulling myself up. The trouble was I had just one functional leg and the good one was significantly weakened because of my fall. As a result I managed to move...just a few millimetres. I tried again...and still made no progress.

I finally decided to give my crutches to Ritchie and clamber my way up. I could see that the face of the rocks in this section were almost smoothly vertical, and there were hardly any footholds or handholds. My knee had almost given way by this time. But I did not have a choice. I started hoisting myself up one step at a time.

Several minutes had passed since I decided to scramble my way to the top of this part of the climb. I was in a lot of pain and nowhere near the end. But the memories of that summer day back in Romania, when I cut my foot going to school, kept me going through the bruised knees and the bleeding palms. Finally, I reached for the hand of one of the local guides at the top of the climb. I had come a little closer to the sun. I had bruises everywhere but somehow, the pain numbed itself for a while as I celebrated the moment quietly.

We continued our ascent until we broke through the clouds and reached the top of the Barranco wall. I looked around as tufts of clouds drifted past us dreamily. The majestic Kibo peak came into view again with its snow-laden summit glistening in the sun. We could also see our next stop, the Karanga valley on the other side. It was a spectacular view and we all sat down for a while to take it all in.

I had rested my crutches against a rock by my side. I started scraping off the layers of mud on them with my pocket knife.

The summit awaited me, just one more day to go. I could not have come this far without my crutches. I picked them up as Ritchie beckoned to start the exploration.

We made our way down the Barranco wall into the Karanga valley. Giant lava rocks scattered the bone-dry floor of the alpine desert landscape. Cracks ran through the ground haphazardly and there were hardly any signs of vegetation. It looked like a chunk of a distant planet but there was an inexplicable beauty in its haunted appearance. Kibo continued to loom over us on the left as we made our way through the barren land.

The loose rock scree made for a tricky descent and I had to put my foot down harder than I usually would, with every single step, just to make sure that I did not slip. I had already tripped too many times before, and it had taken a toll on my knee. I did not want things to get any worse. I still had another day to go.

We were fairly relaxed as the trek had definitely lost some of its harsher nature. We kept going for an hour or so until we ran into another tough, almost vertical climb. Even though easier than the Barranco wall climb, it was still quite a feat to accomplish. I was getting a little tense because the soreness in my knees and shoulders was growing alarmingly. I kept thinking about the day that was to follow, the result of my effort of several months. Failure was not an option that I had even cared to consider from the start, but what if it was something that I could not avoid?

I have lost count of the things that I have failed at. It is a good sign, because I do not hang on to failures. I look forward to new challenges. I could not realize my dream of becoming a footballer. It was a stinging failure that helped to define the way I am. I had to accept it. And it was bitter. And I felt it was unfair. But, the truth is that life was never unfair to me. There was always something else better around the corner waiting for me to discover and use. The negative experiences I have had in my life, have led me to the discovery that everything happens for a good reason – especially the bad, negative things. Those happen, first to teach us something beneficial, and to show us the way to a better option. We will never, unless we are very lucky, see those benefits instantly, but with time we will see the benefit of every negative that happens in our lives. Keep believing that something good is going to happen as a result of this.

When the truth about not being able to become a footballer finally sank in, I turned my attention to another sport - table tennis. And I did manage to be a runner-up in a competition for disabled players, in London. But somehow, I did not feel quite right about being put in a box with a label on it that said 'disabled'. It seemed to be a commentary about my capability or the apparent lack of it perhaps. Why couldn't I compete in a regular event? I am the best judge of how much my disability limits me, not someone else.

I have always loved physical challenges. I would have loved to become a sports professional but I knew that I would never be considered on par with those who are not physically disabled. I would never be a sports professional, I would always be a sport professional with a disability. So I let go. And with that, died another dream, of becoming a swimmer. When I realised that my football dream was not going to happen, I loved being active, so I went for swimming. For a while, I wanted to become a professional swimmer, but when I discovered that you had to have both legs working properly if you wanted to compete at a very high level, I let that go too. However, before I realised that this was going to be another dead dream, I used to go swimming every week. I used to swim for about 2 hours each time, imagining I was competing in a professional competition. Back in 1995 I even got a certificate for swimming 2000 metres uninterrupted. I was very tired, and because this was my first ever certificate of achieving something, I felt amazing, like a real champion. It felt really nice, and I wanted to keep that feeling for as long as possible.

I have chased every one of my dreams until I had nothing more to give. Every single time. Yet, failure was at times, inevitable. I could not become an actor. Or a model. Like most young people who loved to be active all the time, I had dreamed about being an actor as well. I also dreamed of being a professional model too. I tried modelling, for the first time, in 1999. It was a competition for disabled people, held in London. It was a very serious competition – one of the judges was the ex-wife of a very successful rock singer. The winner of that competition was signed up with a professional modelling agency, and a contract with a high-street retailer. I really fancied that idea, and I was hoping to win it. My English was not very good back then, so I didn't do too well when I had to answer the judge's questions. In spite of that, I think I came in second place, but on this occasion the winner took it all. I was very disappointed. When I got back home that evening, I tore apart all of the posters I had in my room. These were posters of people who were, literally, my role models because I used to imagine myself being one of them. That evening I decided to stop my dreams of modelling. I stopped everything that was related to modelling. That was until 2010 after the success of climbing Mt. Kilimanjaro. By chance I came across an advert looking for an ambassador for disabled models. I applied for the role, and when I met up with the founder, she asked me if I wanted to model for them as well. I didn't hesitate for one moment! As a result I managed to feature on one catwalk show at Oxford Fashion Week, and another show for Style and Frock in London. I also featured on one TV advert, which was aired in the USA, and I got one paid modelling assignment for a training company. So, in a way my dream from over 10 years previously did come true, but not to the scale which I really wanted. After a few months of working in the modelling industry, I realised that people were giving me these opportunities because they felt sorry for me. So after a few months I decided that modelling, after all, wasn't for me. Not in this way anyway. I wanted to do and achieve things because I was capable, not because some kind-hearted people wanted to 'help me out'. So I stopped.

I have also tried my luck at acting. Acting was something else that I dreamed of doing when I was young. This again, happened after the Kilimanjaro success. I found a company in London that teaches acting, and I enrolled on one of their beginners courses. I went there my first day. It was great, we had a lot of fun, but at the same time, I could feel that, again, people felt kind of sorry for me and marginalized me a little bit. I have lost count of the things that I have tried and given up. It is a good sign because it means that I have tried a lot of things. I have never pondered over my failures for too long. I have given my failed dreams the farewell they deserved and moved on.

Failures are what you make of them. Mine have always been harbingers of hope and something more; a lot more in fact. Every lost opportunity has made way for something more meaningful. But things have not always made sense. And as I have realized, they don't have to. Sometimes, you just have to accept the absurdity that goes on in your life. You have to wait for that glimmer of hope in the distance, however faint. And when you see it, chase it with all you have. But if you fail to, just tell yourself that there will be more opportunities to come. Tell yourself that there is something much better out there for you.

From my experience I have found that there is a good reason for our failures, for why things don't work out the way we want, wish or hope. The reason is: we are meant to achieve something much more meaningful, much more important and much more significant in our life. These "little failures" are the signposts which show us the way to where we are truly heading; somewhere even bigger and better! Do not get discouraged when something doesn't work out the way we planned or wished. It's the world's way of telling us that we are meant to achieve something even better than what we intended in the first place! Just stay in faith.

I had given my dream of climbing Mt Kilimanjaro everything, and I was willing to continue to give it my all until I saw it through to the end. But I was not sure how much I had left in me. I have always chased my dreams fearlessly; the thought of not succeeding or not making it has never crossed my mind but it did now. And I was not too sure why. Maybe there was too much at stake. I felt that if I gave this up, I would be using my disability as an excuse.

To become a footballer, or an actor, or a model, or a swimmer, I would have had to accept the norms set by others. I would have had to accept their ideas of the limitations that a disabled person has. But there were no such restrictions here. I was climbing this mountain alongside people who were able-bodied. I was facing the same set of challenges that they were facing, every step of the way. The only differences between me and them, were one limp leg and a pair of crutches.

For once, I wanted the questions to stop. I wanted to put all doubts to rest. I knew that even though I was disabled I could still have a normal life. I can be disabled and still do all the things that any other abled-bodied person can do.

Before I went to the boarding school in Cluj-Napoca, I used to attend a regular school with other normal kids. And it seemed natural to me that if I could sit alongside them in a classroom and study, I could do everything else that they could do, even outside the classroom.

I rubbed my sore palms together in an attempt to revive them, adjusted my knee strap and continued walking. This was not going to be another incomplete dream. Not this time.

After lunch, we steadily climbed our way to Barafu camp. The bleak scenery around us was an absolute contrast to the stunning view of both the Kibo and the Mawenzi peaks. The Heim and Kersten glaciers had also come in to view by this point. It was just the most breathtaking sight, and I kept taking it in after every few steps. The short breaks also helped me relax the soreness in my shoulders, palms and knees. I was taking it slowly, trying to save as much energy as I could for the summit night.

The rest of the trek that day was just a long tiring stretch as we kept climbing and scrambling over rocks and boulders before we finally reached camp around nine. I don't remember anything except for the numbing exhaustion I experienced. "The summit awaits...", I thought to myself before I fell into a deep sleep.

Chapter 21

Day 5

My Dream Was Accomplished

"You are never given a dream without also being given the power to make it true. You may have to work for it, however." - **Richard Bach**

Next morning, I woke up at two am. I had only slept for 3-4 hours. We had to start early in order to avoid walking in the sun for too long. I was completely disoriented and tired beyond measure. My knees and shoulders seemed to have become worse. The adrenaline rush of the day before had hidden some of the pain but, this morning, the adrenaline had gone and the pain was back. I was struggling to keep my eyes open. But the summit awaited.

A change of clothes and a bowl of porridge later, I was ready to go; the agony and sleep would have to wait. We all hugged each other and wished each other 'Good Luck', trying to sound cheerful and upbeat despite blood shot, baggy eyes. I kept chanting in my head, "I can do it". Believe, and the magic will follow.

I sipped on my energy drink and strapped on my head torch before walking the steep ascent towards the summit. I was tired and it was pitch dark. I could not see the path ahead of me; the only purpose that the head torch served, was to be a beacon for all kinds of bugs. I could not see where I was placing my crutches; I would place my foot forward only after tapping the surface once or twice with my crutches to make sure that it was safe to do so.

I was feeling very drowsy and a sharp pain was already spreading quickly up my neck. It was extremely cold and I could feel my skin breaking into goose bumps under layers of clothing. My knees and shoulders were completely jammed and one hour into the trek, I was seizing up like a car engine without oil.

I had fallen twice already and things were just getting worse. My mental strength was ebbing away very rapidly as my muscles seemed to be shouting "Stop, stop, stop, we can't take it anymore!". At one point, my palms just froze and my fingers would not bend to hold the crutches. My head was spinning and I was completely out of breath. "I can't go on, I am done", I thought to myself.

The porters were singing and shouting to keep our spirits up but it was just adding to my troubles. My headache was only getting sharper every time I heard their screams. I just needed some peace and quiet. I could not see where I was headed and my body had just given up.

Everyone was suffering in the intense cold. Our faces were contorting in weird ways and our hands were trembling. The was hardly and conversations , because everyone's teeth were chattering so badly. Our bodies were caught in a fierce battle with the cold.

It took me a long while to get accustomed to this new life. It was extremely difficult but it made me tough and independent. It made me what I am today. As the cloud created by my breath cleared, I looked down at my hands, I could barely move my fingers; "Just like old times!", I thought to myself. This really reminded me of the old times when I was in the boarding school in Romania, cleaning the grounds in the freezing cold temperatures outside. Negative thoughts were starting to creep in, but I very quickly turned my attention of where I was placing my crutches.

I kept going with the help of all the amazing people in my team who kept my spirits up. The porters especially, supported me, as well as the rest of the team.

But I was still struggling. As we kept gaining altitude, I kept getting out of breath. I still could not see a thing. And I kept falling over. How could I continue on a path that I could barely see? But my belief kept me going.

And when my belief felt threatened, I kept turning back the pages of my life, to remember moments of joy and kindness, and people who had made my life beautiful. Whatever incentives the summit held for me, it held happiness, and a lot of it. And I wanted to remind myself how it would feel when I reached the top. And how that one moment of sheer joy would just erase the pain that lead up to it.

My knee twitched violently as I tried to step over a huge boulder and I was forced to take a break so that the pain could perhaps settle down. As I took another sip from my energy drink, and tried to calm myself down, I kept imagining the feeling I had when I got my first Christmas present. And then I pictured myself on the summit, and I could imagine the same feelings of excitement and happiness inside, and a familiar warmth spreading through me. I needed to go on and endure what I had to, in order to experience those wonderful feelings of joy.

The darkness around us completely hid the path we were following. Or trying to follow. It seemed like a crazy thing to climb a mountain in darkness. Even more crazily, the darkness was going to lead us into the light.

The sun was starting to wake up, and as its first rays reached me, I heaved a sigh of relief as the warmth soothed my tired body. We were getting closer to the sun. We were getting closer to the summit.

We took a short break to recharge ourselves and I took the opportunity to look around. It suddenly hit me that we were way up high on the mountain. Whoever came up with the phrase "The world at my feet", must have been here when he first thought about it.

I was stunned by the breathtaking beauty that surrounded me. A bright blue sky, the freshness of the morning sun, and its warmth raging on against the freezing temperatures...I was utterly overwhelmed by the tranquility of the moment. I could have endured all the pain that I had, twice over, just for this view.

I calmed down. I started breathing evenly again. The wonderful scenery worked its magic deep inside me. I was filled with gratitude for the wonders of nature around me, and for the richness of my life. I was humbled.

We continued to climb as the sun rose higher in the sky. The ascent became steeper and steeper. The higher we went the thinner the air became and, as that happened, it became harder to breathe. With every step I took, I was getting closer to the summit. Yet, it felt like I had only just begun. The snow-covered ground was slippery and it was becoming more difficult to find a firm place to put my crutches and my feet.

At one point, I turned around and I saw the trail that I had left behind - a footprint and two small circles, the base of my crutches. "Embrace the gift of not being what everyone else is", I reminded myself.

I reached the crater rim at Stella point, at a height of 5793 metres around eight in the morning. I was beyond exhausted; my right foot and palms were completely numb from the pressure that I put on them while using my crutches. I felt like I was hung over due to lack of sleep. In spite of the amazing scenery around me, exhaustion was taking over and numbing my senses.

By the time I reached Stella point, Ritchie and his group were having tea, prepared by the porters. How did they do it? They constantly amazed us with their skills and abilities to innovate in difficult conditions. I had, and still have, total admiration for them. So, here I was at Stella point drinking a wonderful warm cup of tea – I don't know how they managed, and I don't care – it was just wonderful. I can swear that I have never tasted a better cup of tea and a biscuit in my entire life. Although on second thoughts, a hot cup of water would have tasted as good, given my state. "Just an hour or two more to go", I reminded myself.

I started walking again. I waded through the snow, breathing laboriously, each step kept getting harder than the last - a little higher, a little colder, a little more painful. I wanted to take in the scenery around me - the glistening glaciers, the delightful clear sky, the fresh air and the enormity of the fact that I was going to make it. I was going to make it after all the dreadful moments of despair and hopelessness.

But I had to keep moving, because I was certain that my body was going to give up soon. And now that I was getting so close to the summit, I realized that I would only be half way through my journey when I got there: I still had to get down to the bottom again! I considered the descent and how I would do it. And I had absolutely no idea! Still, I would sort that problem out in due course – right now I was on the way up!

I kept wading through the snow somehow; any moment now, I was going to collapse. I was running out of everything that had helped me get here - my belief, faith, motivation. My eyes were holding on to the promise of the sight of the peak, even as my body and mind were letting go. I kept going though. I kept telling myself that I can do it. I kept on ignoring the physical pain, but I had to stop quite often as the pain was quite unbearable. Somehow I managed to convince my mind that if I still move, no matter how slow, I will reach the top.

I was in the middle of what can only be defined as divine beauty. And I was at the point of finding something that would change my life, and become my legacy. I was just two hours away from achieving my dream and redefining the view that so many people had about what I was capable of.

At last, I had my first glimpse of the summit two hours later. Was it two hours or two days? I could no longer tell. As I approached the peak I could see people from the other group already at the summit, absolutely jubilant and the smiles on their faces defying any kind of pain or agony.

I finally reached Uhuru peak at an altitude of 5895 metres. I could not understand immediately what had happened. Everyone was hugging and congratulating each other, laughing and crying at the same time. I was blank. And then suddenly, every part of me rushed to fill the void. Relief drenched me as tears set themselves free. I had made it!

I had defied the overwhelming gravity of reason - How could a disabled guy climb a mountain? I had done what I was not capable of. Or so it seemed, before that moment. An inexplicable warmth soaked me, submerging the brutality that I had endured for several days.

But would my life change after this? Would well-meaning people stop asking questions about why I was on crutches, and would they stop expecting me to be not very good at doing physical things? And would I stop being that guy on crutches? No, I was sure that the questions would continue for life. It was then that I asked myself "So what was the point of doing all of this?" And the answer came back, loud and clear, "All of us have to push ourselves to breaking point if we want to discover our strengths. There is no other way".

I thought I had nothing left in me by the time I made it to the summit. I was so exhausted that it felt like I had lost everything. But then all of the hopes, faith, dreams came back....everything. "If I can do this, I can do anything. I can be everything that I think I can", a voice at the back of my head told me. "Yes, indeed."

The greatest odds are those that we stack up against ourselves. And the biggest victory is one that we win by overcoming those odds. We all have moments of doubt about what we are capable of, and sometimes, that is what kills our dreams, the thought that we cannot do it. I had as many moments of doubt as certainty, while climbing the mountain.

But of all the things that I felt I needed to overcome - people who ridiculed me, people who did not believe in me, the nature of the challenge itself...the hardest things to overcome were my own moments of doubt that I could not do it. But I had finally found the courage to prove myself wrong. I was finally at peace with myself.

"Congratulations!", the guy who had been mean to me at the bottom, broke my chain of thoughts. Then he hugged me. "The day I saw you at the airport, I was certain that you would never make it to the top. As we climbed higher, I was finding it very difficult, and I almost gave up. Then I looked at you Vas. I asked myself how a disabled guy could be climbing this mountain when I, an able-bodied fellow, was struggling. When I was getting weaker, I looked at you for inspiration. I am here because of you. Thanks", he said. We complete ourselves by completing others. Yes, it all made sense now.

Chapter 22

Day 5, 9:00 AM

Exhausted and Numb

*"I firmly believe that any man's finest hour, the greatest fulfilment of all that he holds dear, is that moment when he has worked his heart out in a good cause and lies exhausted on the field of battle - victorious." - **Vince Lombardi***

Part of me felt numb, part of me felt exhausted, but part of me could not yet realise that I had just accomplished one of my significant dreams. I just wanted time to stop.

Our team was supposed to gather at Stella Point before we started the descent. Dazed, exhausted and in tremendous pain, I somehow made my way back.

"We are going to make our way back to Millennium camp which is about 13000 metres from here. We will stop for breakfast at Barafu camp...". I stopped hearing after 13000 metres really. I was not going to make it. My body was breaking down. And the heat was getting harsher by the minute.

I voiced my concerns to Ritchie and Jo, and it was decided that I would be taken down by the porters. I was assigned three porters. One of them took my crutches, the second, my rucksack, and the third one took me! He simply carried me on his back. And we made our way back to Barafu camp for breakfast.

The three porters were amazing individuals. They kept my spirits up with their friendly chatter and even though I was barely conscious, I could imagine the effort it must have taken to carry me all the way to Barafu camp. Their positive attitude reminded me of my family back home.

The porters were just as positive as my brother and sisters had been. I felt like I was amongst my own people who did not look down on me in my moment of weakness. I will forever be grateful to those three porters for their kindness and their ability to make me feel safe and happy.

After breakfast at Barafu camp, I decided to carry on, on my own. I was still suffering quite badly from a stinging pain that affected my palms, arms and right foot.

Two pairs of gloves, two layers of plaster on my palms and half a dozen stops to layer my right foot with plasters could do nothing to ease the discomfort. I kept taking off my boot every few steps in a desperate attempt to make the pain bearable. I was tired from using the crutches. I could not feel my arms anymore.

On one of my usual breaks, I decided to take my gloves off. I experienced an alarming numbness in the little finger of my right hand. I could not move it either. The numbness started from my finger and traced a path all the way down to my lower back. I had once experienced something similar before from a battered nerve under my armpit due to excessive use of crutches. I did not think any further about how much worse it could get. It was a scary thought. I put my gloves back on and had a word with Ritchie about it.

I was going to be carried by the porters again. But this time, in a makeshift stretcher made out of sack. It had been raining and the slippery ground was not a great setting for me being carried on someone's back.

We reached Millennium camp at seven in the evening. Dinner followed, and then the much needed sleep.

Chapter 23

Day 6

Our Last Day on Mt. Kilimanjaro

"My footprint on its snow covered peak would soon disappear, but the imprint it had left on me would stay forever." - **Vasile Onica**

This was our last day on the mountain.

Soon after breakfast, the porters gathered to give us a farewell which was an extremely emotional affair for everyone. We would not have made it without them. None of us. We hugged and shook hands and then headed down to Mweka gate.

A gentle 10 kms trek took us to Mweka gate through an exquisite rainforest trail. I was again carried by the porters all the way down to Mweka gate.

A few formalities, some more final goodbyes and hugs and beers later, we were on our way back to Moshi town. Time had moved very slowly while we were on the mountain. Or so it had seemed. But now that I looked back, I realized that it had gone by too fast.

I had made it and discovered a place to fit in, something that gave meaning to my existence. I was thinking about the charity that I had raised funds for.

And the people that I would be able to help as a result.

I caught a glimpse of Mt Kilimanjaro from my window seat in the minibus that was taking us back to our hotel. I looked at its immense body and its snow covered peak, one little tear surfaced from my tired eyes. I had been there. My footprint on its snow covered peak would soon disappear, but the imprint it had left on me would stay forever. I smiled and closed my eyes. I was at peace.

All the efforts I had put into this dream, for the last eight months, had been well worth it!

Now I had to dream another dream...

Chapter 24

<u>Work In Progress</u>

"I will always have to strive to be what I can become." -
Vasile Onica

Triiiinnng! The alarm chimes. It is 6:30 in the morning. It has been a few years since I climbed Mt Kilimanjaro. And even though my life has fallen back into the same routine, there is something within me that has changed. I believe in myself a lot more than I used to. And I live every moment of my life trying to make it more meaningful, even when doing the most minor things. I am grateful for this life, and I am grateful for every opportunity that has come my way, and the ones that wait for me in the future.

But I cannot spend my entire life with the memories of one achievement. There is lot more to be done, because I have not reached the peak of what I can become. And I do not think I ever will. It gives me sleepless nights. So, I will keep challenging myself. Because every time I achieve something everyone else thought I could not, I discover that I have so much more within me waiting to be discovered. Every time, I stand on the verge of questioning myself and breaking apart, I find answers to questions that I have never asked before. I have many more mountains to climb. I will never know all that I am capable of unless I push my boundaries further.

The need to maintain status quo does not define me. It should not define you either. We have many more dreams to dream.

And yet, my achievements do not define me either, not in the eyes of the world at least. No matter how many mountains I climb, there will always be someone who will have doubts about what I stand for and what I am capable of achieving. Every single one of us has those doubters. The 'secret' is not to prove them wrong, but to prove yourself right; that you are worthy and capable of achieving your dreams. Every challenge is a journey to put those doubts to rest. Every achievement is a journey forgotten readily. I will never be done. I will always be a work in progress. I will always have to strive to be what I can become.

I have fallen countless times. But I have got back on my feet every single time. It has been really hard and it will always be. My life is not a fairy tale. But I will still have my happy ending, and I believe you will too!

"These then are my last words to you. Be not afraid of life. Believe that life is worth living and your belief will help create the fact." – William James

Final Word

I hope that you have enjoyed this book. I also hope that it has inspired and motivated you to take action, to turn your dreams and ambitions into reality.

So, what is your dream?

What is it that you always wanted to do, but never did?

Why did you not do it?

We usually don't go for our dreams because we think that other people will ridicule us; we assume that our dreams are too small, insignificant or that they are too big to be put into practice.

The worse thing is that we worry too much about what others will think. Even worse than that is the belief that we are not worthy enough to achieve our dreams and goals. I am here to tell you that you are worthy of all the good things in life! You were born worthy, that's why you are here, on this planet!

I encourage you to, first, write down that thing (or things) which you really want to do, be or have. Go' on, just get a piece of paper and a pen, and write it down.

Don't worry if that which you want to achieve is too small or too big. Don't worry about what others will think. This is your dream, your life – live it.

If you have people in your life who are negative and sceptical – don't tell them about your dream(s). Whatever you do, just take that first step, and believe in your powers to make your dream a reality.

The reason you have dreams is because you are capable of making them a reality!

And, as Ralph Waldo Emerson said; once you make a decision, the universe conspires to make it happen.

Make the decision to turn your dreams into reality.

I believe you can do it!

I know you can do it!

I will be more than happy to hear your success stories, so please get in touch with me.

You can contact me at:

My facebook page: www.facebook.com/vas.onica

E-mail: vasnic@hotmail.com

My blog: www.livelifenlaugh.com or www.livelifenlaugh.co.uk